PRAISE FOR F. ...

"Together with the novels of Graham Gre ... Conrad, Han Suyin, Yukio Mishima, F. Sionil Jose ... is one of the top ten novels written on Southeast Asia."

— *RON RENNARD*, Discovery Magazine

"(*Ermita*)—beautiful, moving. He belongs to the vernacular tradition of searing social criticism."

— *BIENVENIDO LUMBERA*, Critic

"If we had to choose only one set of literary texts to represent the 20th century it (Rosales Saga) may be the only prose epic of our time."

— *ISAGANI R. CRUZ,* Playwright, critic

"...taken together, (the Rosales novels) are the most impressive legacy of any writer to Philippine culture."

— *RICAREDO DEMETILLO*, Poet and Critic

"His touch with language is rivaled, perhaps, only by N.V.M. Gonzalez or Nick Joaquin...and his stories are moving portraits of Filipino society."

— *JOSEPH A. GALDON*, Ateneo de Manila University

"...Like Dickens, Jose is a master storyteller, breeding characters from setting and social condition. Like Donne, Jose is a poet, seeking the spiritual ramifications of his subjects. (In *Don Vicente*) so powerful is Jose's sense of soul that he infuses not only his characters with it, but his readers as well."

— The Baltimore Sun

"*Dusk* demonstrates why many claim that Jose could be the first Filipino writer to win the Nobel Prize... Highly recommended."

— *FAYE A. CHADWELL*, Library Journal

"Jose writes English prose with a passion that, at its best moments, transcends the immediate scene. He is a masterful short story writer."

— *CHRISTINE CHAPMAN* International Herald Tribune

"Francisco Sionil Jose, Asia's white hope (or tan stand?) for the Nobel, has been translated into every major language, including the Scandinavian, and is, hands down, the most widely read Filipino author."

— *NICK JOAQUIN*, National Artist

"F. Sionil Jose could become the first Filipino to win the Nobel Prize for literature...he's a fine writer and it would be welcome recognition of cultural achievement in his troubled country. (He) is widely known and acclaimed in Asia."

— *JOHN GRIFFIN*, The Honolulu Advertiser

"America has no counterpart...no one who is simultaneously a prolific novelist, a social and political organizer, an editor and a journalist, a small-scale entrepreneur... As a writer, Jose is famous for two bodies of work. One is the Rosales sequence, a set of five novels published over a twenty-year span which has become a kind of national saga."

— *JAMES FALLOWS* , The Atlantic

"Jose is one of Asia's most eminent writers and novelists. His passionate, sometimes transcendent writings illuminate contemporary Filipino life in graceful and historically anchored narratives of power brokers and the brokered, of landowners and the indentured."

— *SCOTT RUTHERFORD*, Islands Magazine

"In Filipino literature in recent years, the creative work of Francisco Sionil Jose occupies a special place... Jose is great artist."

— *IGOR PODBEREZSKY,* Institute of Oriental Studies, Moscow

"The reader of this slim volume of well-crafted stories *(Three Filipino Women)* will learn more about the Philippines, its people and its concerns than from any journalistic account or from a holiday trip there. Jose's book takes us to the heart of the Filipino mind and soul, to the strengths and weaknesses of its men, women and culture."

— *LYNNE BUNDESEN,* Los Angeles Times

"*The Samsons* is more than a story; it is art. Pepe Samson's self actualization is one of the most beautiful transformation in literature. Jose creates a river of language."

—*ASHLEY REYNOLDS,* The Decatur Daily

"Sionil Jose has the ability to write evocatively...his description of the rural environment have as intense glow and a lyrical shine... Linguistically and artistically he has developed his craft and is now the complete master of an American style...he is no longer an author depending on a language and psychology whose origins are in colonialism but is truly an emancipated stylist, an interpreter of character and analyst of society."

— *ARTHUR LUNDKVIST*, The Swedish Academy,
Svenska Dagbladet, Stockholm

"...Jose never flattens his characters in the service of rhetoric... Even more impressive is Jose's ability to tell important stories in lucid, but never merely simple prose...it's refreshing to see a politically engaged writer who dares to reach for a broader audience."

— *LAURE MILLER*, San Francisco Chronicle

"His stories truly carry the reader into the petty, debilitating, nepotistic, and often nightmarish world of politics and power."

— *DAVID McELVEEN*, Asiaweek (Hong Kong)

"Seldom has a writer reflected so well the qualities and the failing of his people. Francisco Sionil Jose is one of the best-known writers in his country and abroad. He crossed this century embracing the hopes and the disillusions of his land: his essays and his articles as well as his novels are inseparable from the modern history of the Philippines."

— *PHILIPPE PONS,* Le Monde des livres, Paris

"Tolstoy himself, not to mention Italo Svevo, would envy the author of this story... This short...scorching work whets our appetite for Sionil Jose's masterpiece, the five-novel Rosales Saga."

— *JOSEPH COATES*, Chicago Tribune

"F. Sionil Jose writes with an urgency that recalls D.H. Lawrence and preoccupations resembling those of Hemingway. (His) prose has, at its best sustained intensity that is highly impressive. His work is as part, an important part, of the Filipinos' search for a nobler sense of themselves."

— *DAVID BURLEIGH*, Mainichi Daily News, Tokyo

"No Filipino novelist in English has written as adeptly, movingly, and in a language that is its own sole, freshly created universe about the Filipino's quest for a just moral order. Jose's fiction—limn and define a shining vision of today's Filipino: a future that is more fair, more just, more caring and ultimately more creative."

—*EDITORIAL*, Philippine Daily Inquirer

"Jose's collection is an incisive comment on the Philippines' powerful matriarchal foundation. His reputation was built largely on the marvelous Rosales Saga—a series of novels published in the Philippines spanning nearly a century—*Three Filipino Women* represents slight shift...a contemporary, introspective, and quieter work, where history and politics—the manipulation and oppression of the poor by generations of elites—although present, are less pronounced."

— *PETER BACHO,* The Christian Science Monitor

"I read Jose Rizal and F. Sionil Jose before I came here (Manila). Those are the only Filipino writers I could find that are translated."

— *DR. PATCH ADAMS*, Philipine Daily Inquirer

"...an Oriental Gorky...the pen of this literary giant produced a rich harvest...the difficult birth of a forgotten people."

— *ANDRE CLAVEL*, L'Express, Paris

"(Jose) an outstanding saga writer. If ever a Nobel Prize in literature will be awarded to a Southeast Asian writer, it will be F. Sionil Jose..."

— The Mainichi Shimbun (Tokyo)

"Considered by many to be Asia's most likely candidate for the Nobel Prize for Literature."

— The Singapore Straits Times

"Readers will be tantalized by these glimpses of lives... Jose's elegiac tone complements his narratives..."

— Publishers Weekly

"This great Philippine novel takes place within two critical decades... *Dusk*, with its transitional fusing of dark with light, is possessed of a grand brooding material and metaphoric immanence that seems to guide all of Sionil Jose's work."

— *REAMY JANSEN*, The Bloomsburry Review

THREE FILIPINO WOMEN

F. Sionil José

Solidaridad Publishing House
531 Padre Faura, Ermita
Manila, Philippines

FOR

Mochtar Lubis,
Sulak Sivaraksa and
Marcos C. Roces

All the characters in this novel are real
only in the reader's imagination.

Second Printing, 2003
Published by
Solidaridad Publishing House
531 Padre Faura, Ermita
Manila, Philippines

ISBN 971-8845-29-1

Cadena de Amor

ONE

In the preparation of my study on Narita Reyes, I am indebted to my colleagues, particularly to my former teachers, Professors Alejo Orina and M. D. Guerzon who read the manuscript and gave valuable advice. I am also grateful to my typist and secretary, T. Jovel, who transcribed most of the tapes, changed my "alright" to "all right," and kept the door closed to all sorts of noise. And last but not least, I am grateful to the Narita Reyes Foundation for its generous support that allowed me a trip to the United States for research and interviews, and provided for the publication of the political biography of a woman whose personality has considerably altered our view of domestic politics during the last decade.

When I started this project, I was faced with the problem of objectivity. I had known Narita all my life and if I just hewed closely to what is observable data and behavior, I would do injustice to a woman who was far more complex than those personality profiles that the mass media presented. There was much more in what Narita did as compared to what she said; she was sparing in her words and let her actions speak instead.

This much shorter narrative is a spin-off, different from the lengthier and documented original. Nevertheless, with this format, I hope to present one of the most unusual personalities in contemporary Filipino society, in all her scintillating uniqueness.

I have always admired Narita Reyes even though at times it had to be from a distance. As is often said, *Ligaw tingin, kantot hangin* (courtship by looking, fucking the wind). One reason for this is that she made me feel inferior, a result I think of the fact that when we were in grade school, though we were of the same age, she was taller than I was. It was a feeling which persisted through the years, vanquished only in those rare instances when I could physically express my fondness for her.

Narita was an only child and she lived with her *mestizo* (half-breed) parents in a small house roofed with rusting tin across the street from ours. Their house which had a brick wall was once the kitchen—all that was left of a much more substantial house that had burned down. The ruins still stood in the wide lot fenced with brick that had fallen apart in places. Her grandfather was once a wealthy landlord but had lost his lands because of gambling and women; all that remained was the wide lot overgrown with weeds, with pomelo and guava trees which hid their house from view. Narita's father clerked in the municipal building while her mother sold meat in the market, and when Narita was not in school, she helped her mother run the stall.

Narita and I were both Sagittarians; we were born almost to the minute, in the wee hours of the morning of November 30, 1933. Father, who made the deliveries, said it was a hectic dawn—what with him having to rush from our house to theirs and back.

Narita was often in our house for, like me, she liked to read. Father's library included a set of *The Book of Knowledge,* some novels, back issues of *The National Geographic* and other magazines. I was always playing in their wide, weed-choked yard, too, particularly when the guava and pomelo trees started bearing fruit. During the early days of the war, in 1942, her family evacuated with us to our farm in Bogo which was about three kilometers from the town. We did not stay there long; we need not have left town for the Japanese never came to Santa Ana in force except for occasional patrols. As a matter of fact, Santa Ana is quite isolated from the rest of the country and progress really never seemed to have touched it—till Narita came and blazed through in a way Santa Ana will never see again.

For one, the land in our part of the island is rocky and the mountains always seemed to loom closer as the irrevocable margin beyond which our cane fields could not encroach. We depended on the rain for irrigation and sometimes, it was niggardly. And because the land is poor, we never had the largesse that the Silay and Bacolod people enjoyed. In fact, Bacolod could seem as distant as Manila although it is only sixty kilometers away and the only people who went there regularly were men like Father who had business at the provincial hospital or with the drug companies.

Narita could be very quiet. We could be with those books without speaking for hours; yet afterwards, people thought she was a compulsive talker. This was unfair for in later years she could be a patient listener even to the loudest braggart, as if she were hearing words of pure wisdom when they were pretentious drivel—as they often were when most of the politicians she knew wanted to be identified as pious nationalists.

She was in Grade II when she became champion declaimer with her tearful rendition of "The boy stood on the burning deck . . ." When she was in Grade VI, she was chosen the best singer with her "Lahat ng Araw" ("All of My Days")—a song she made very popular later. Her voice was scarcely trained but she could render a song better than most of the young singers on radio and TV today because Narita had style.

Even when we were still in school, it was already obvious that she was beautiful and talented but because we were neighbors, I took her for granted. We played a lot, in whatever season. When the rains came and brought green to the fields, we would be there, catching grasshoppers. And at dusk, we looked for spiders in the bushes, in the profusion of cadena de amor that clambered over the brick walls and bloomed in white and pink. There was a particular species of spider that we found among the vines, the one with long limbs and a very small body. It was a good fighter. We would position the spiders on each end of a coconut midrib, watch them inch towards the center and once there, they would grapple and bite each other. The loser was soon rendered immobile and coated with the silky strands that trailed from them. Never was defeat so complete and final.

Narita's mother supplied us with meat and Mother said she was trustworthy; she gave us the best sections and told us if it was carabao or beef unlike other butchers who cheated their customers. I took this as a matter of course; after all, Father did not charge them for his services.

Their house was always in disarray—a characteristic that Narita did not bring with her later: their clothes all over the place, the bamboo floor already rotting in places, the dishes unwashed in the basin in the kitchen. But there were plants everywhere for Narita loved to grow them, even the weeds in the yard, I think. It was as if by some arcadian magic, she could transform an ordinary place into lush green. She had the touch of life.

When we were in Grade VI, I made a "mark" on Narita. We were playing that Saturday morning in their wide yard. She was then tomboyish and it was not unusual for her to beat me in running, jumping and that morning, basketball. She had rigged up a hoop on one side of their house, up the brick wall. I accidentally pushed her and she stumbled and banged her chin against a rusty piece of iron in the woodwork. When she turned to me, although she was laughing, there was blood on her chin. It turned out to be an ugly wound and, with her handkerchief staunching it, we went to Father who was in his clinic in the ground floor of our house. He looked at the wound, gave her anaesthesia, then sewed it in two stitches all the while asking how it had happened. Narita did not cry, wince or scream as I would have done with all that pain and blood.

"Brave girl," Father said.

He wanted to see what it was that had cut her so we went back to their yard and when Father saw it, he said, "I'd better give you anti-tetanus serum."

A general practitioner, Father tried to make do without the sophisticated equipment of hospitals but he was always careful. I remember him telling me that about eighty percent of human ailments could be naturally cured by the body without the assistance of either medicines or doctors. But tetanus is tetanus. He decided to have an allergy test first, just giving Narita a bit of injection under the skin. Within seconds she had turned bluish, her eyes dilated and she fell into a faint.

Father blanched. Fortunately, he was prepared for such emergencies. He immediately gave her an anti-allergy shot and when she revived she described how strange she felt and how suddenly everything started to blur and turn black.

"You are allergic to anti-tetanus serum," Father said gravely. "I hope you will not forget that . . ."

I felt guilty and sad for her because her face was disfigured but she just laughed. When the wound healed, there was an indention where the scab had lifted and, in time, the scar itself disappeared. She has had that cleft chin since and, as she herself said, she looked prettier with it.

As an only child, Narita had plenty of time to be alone

and it was only later that I learned how much of this time was spent in reverie, daydreams about going away, far away from Santa Ana and its numbing constrictions.

She did not have pets except a big, white cat. She starved the animal once when she came upon a nest of mice in their yard. She placed the hungry cat in a wire-mesh cage where once her father kept his fighting cocks. Then she brought out two of the grown-up mice and put them in the cage. I shudder every time I recall how she sat before that cage, her eyes impassive but alert, watching the cat pounce on the poor, shrieking rodents.

"It is the way of the world, Eddie," she told me years later when I recalled this. "The strong tearing apart the weak . . ."

As a boy, I was wary of some of the things Narita wanted me to do no matter how easy or innocuous they seemed. One April afternoon we were in the weedy section of their wide yard. The pomelo trees were laden with ripening fruit and she pointed to a rise in the ground as the best place for me to stand so that I could reach the big oranges that dangled over our heads. I went up the low mound without question only to run from it immediately for a host of giant red ants were all over my legs and biting me. It was an anthill that she had told me to stand on. I was on the verge of tears and she broke out laughing at my misery. I forgave her for this.

We were together again from first year to senior year in the local high school. I cannot say honestly that I did not have any feelings for Narita other than those shared by two childhood friends. Such feelings, however, were dampened by the fact that she had grown taller than I.

By this time, too, she started to confide to me those things which even my sisters did not tell me: how it was when she had her first menstruation, how it felt when her breasts started growing, how itchy they were that she had to put plaster bands on them, personal things which, in retrospect, seem to have been the basis of our relationship.

I remember that day the girls wore their gala uniform—white with blue collar—the school colors. It was the school's Foundation Day and, as usual, it was Narita who led the singing of the national anthem. When she got up from her seat, there it was for all to see, the red smudge on her behind. There was twittering among the girls and I had a good mind to go tell her that the menstrual blood had dripped right through. And that was what I did when we filed out of the hall. But she whispered into my ear, her eyes filled with laughter, "I am not due till the fifteenth—as if you didn't know! That's just pig blood—I sat on it early this morning in Mama's stall."

When we were in our senior year, as everyone expected, she became the queen during our High School Day. She had bloomed. I am sure there were men in town who went to her mother's stall just to look at her. She also sang in the church choir regularly and one could always pick out that rich, mellow voice; she did not linger long in the high notes but she could maintain her voice in the higher reaches. I beat her in literature and history but she was better than I was in math, in philosophy and physics, "the subjects that mattered."

Before she became high school queen, her father, who had by then taken to drinking and gambling, became very ill and would have died had not Father taken him to the provincial hospital; it was a rather complicated move. Knowing how government was, Father got a letter from Senator Reyes, builder of the hospital and one of the richest and most powerful men in the country. The senator came from our province and Father knew him.

In a way, we had always been entwined with their lives.

Don Carlos—her father loved being called that though there was nothing affluent or distinguished about him—stayed for quite a time in the hospital with all sorts of complications of the liver, the heart, and whatever else can ravage a man who has indulged and abused himself.

"All the meat in the market and all the money in the municipal treasury," my mother used to say, "cannot pay for the bills."

We wondered where they would get the money but as luck would have it, Senator Reyes stood by them and for a very good reason. When he came to Santa Ana to crown our high school queen, he had brought along his youngest and only living son, Lopito, who was then in his early thirties. Lopito looked at Narita once and did not care for anything after that but to have the beautiful virgin as his wife. Senator Reyes was more circumspect. The girl's personality satisfied him but he wanted to know more about her and her background. This was readily supplied by Father and others in the town whom he had questioned. It was no secret then that when Narita finished high school, great things would be in store for her.

I did not like it: Lopito barging into our street in his fancy sports car, with his driver honking before the old battered house, and Narita coming out all smiles; and their driving together, raising billows of dust as they went to the beach or wherever their fancy took them while her father lay dying in the hospital and her mother toiled in the meat stall. It would have been better if they married but Senator Reyes had other ideas—they would not marry till she finished college.

I left for Manila in a black mood one April morning, a week after we had graduated from high school. Narita was valedictorian. She had delivered the graduation address with feeling, saying it was time for all of us to part, and Senator

Reyes who had come again to give the commencement address had looked at her with pride. In the audience, all of us knew what would happen, that she would go to Manila, too, and be his daughter-in-law. And, years later, I was to realize why Senator Reyes had banked so much on her. Of his four sons only the youngest, Lopito, was alive; two had died and one, an artist, had disappeared in Europe. His two girls had married badly in spite of the fact that their husbands were handpicked by the old man. From all appearances, Senator Reyes had wanted to build a dynasty, as was the practice of most politicians, but had failed. He was not a great believer in heredity. After all, he had often said that it was brains that determined survival and triumph, and he unerringly saw all the virtues that he sought in Narita.

I could not leave without saying good-bye. She was in the yard sweeping the dry leaves of the pomelo trees and she asked me to stay a while. I felt very depressed.

I demurred.

"Well," she said, her eyes crinkling in a smile. "Aren't we friends anymore?"

"I wouldn't want Lopito to say I am using some of your time," I said finally. "I have already said good-bye. "

She pulled me to the bamboo bench by the gate and we sat there. She had on a cheap, printed blue dress and wooden shoes. I could glory forever in her nearness.

"If I didn't know you, I'd think you were jealous."

"Of course not." I glared at her. "How can I be jealous? How can . . ."

She caressed my face with her hand. I brushed it away.

"You are in love with me!" she exclaimed. "Eduardo Cortez. You—in love with me!"

"And if I am," I said, "is that something to despise?"

She caressed my face again and this time, I let her, feeling her rough palm, all resentment gone. Then she held my hand. "But Eddie—you know it cannot be. I will not permit it. We grew up together. Remember how we used to run naked in the rain?" She was looking at me, her big, bright eyes brighter yet, the mischief in them coming through. "And remember this?" She pointed to the cleft in her chin. I smiled with memory and this warm, aching desire to hold her.

"You should be happy that you won't be stuck with me," she continued. "There is no mystery about me. I am open to you as you are to yourself. And marriage is something else—a kind of discovery every day . . ."

"Bullshit," I said. "What is so mysterious about Lopito and his millions?"

The moment I said it, I was sorry, but Narita did not look away and her expression did not change.

"Eddie—you are so unfair. But I forgive you because you are in love with me. Look at it this way. We are in debt to them. Without Lopito, I would be stuck with this." She cast a glance around her, at the bedraggled yard, the dilapidated house, the cadena de amor dying and brown on the brick wall.

Mother visited me at the dorm in Diliman a week after school opened. She brought the news that Narita's father had died, that her mother was now alone in the house together with a niece and still minding the meat stall and that Narita was in Manila, staying at the Assumption Convent to finish college as arranged by Senator Reyes. She had asked where I was, Mother said, and was given my dorm address.

Sure enough, within the week, a note from her arrived. I knew her penmanship, the strong crosses of the *t*'s, the forceful upsweep of the last letter. I had developed early enough habits of the collector and the scholar and I kept that note as well as the other notes that she passed on to me.

Hello Eddie,

You were not with us when Papa died, but I forgive you because you did not know. You did not have to hurry to Manila so early, whatever your reason, but I also understand that. I promised myself I would not be jealous of your girlfriend. I will major in political science and economics, but I don't know if this school has the right teachers for me. I would like to be in your campus, but I should be here for this is a wicked city and I need protection. Please come and see me. I want someone to talk with. The girls here know nothing and I am bored most of the time. Will you do this as a favor?

Affectionately,
N

She always signed her letters to close friends with her initial. I did visit her once at Assumption but that was to escort my sisters there when they finally came to Manila. She did come twice to my dorm and my roommate and acquaintances were agog over the prettiest girl they had ever seen coming to visit wretched me.

My parents came to see me every so often and when my two younger sisters started going to college, Father thought it best to build a house in Manila which, in the long run, would save us money and also be a good investment. He bought a lot in Quezon City and we moved to the house within six months, with Mother commuting to Manila to keep two households. She brought back stories of home, of Narita's mother finally closing her stall and just staying home, of Narita going to the old hometown with Lopito.

Narita visited us and stayed in the house for a night but I was out doing a field survey in Bulacan. When I returned, my sisters told me that when she arrived she was in tears. She had gotten a full scholarship, was tops in her class and would probably graduate *summa*, was taking singing lessons besides, and acting in the musical which the school was presenting. But these were not enough. Her schoolmates from Negros ignored her and did not even ask her to participate in the annual Kahirup Ball—the sugar bloc's most lavish social event of the year.

Senator Reyes did not have enough empathy to see to it that his prospective daughter-in-law should be in it and Narita was too proud to ask. She had, perhaps, thought that simply being pretty and talented would be enough to get her accepted into the snootiest Negros circle.

She did not want to stay in the college dorm that night. She had an "important social engagement," too, even if it meant sulking in an anonymous middle-class home in Quezon City.

Narita must have gloated when, shortly after the Kahirup snub, she appeared on the cover of the *Women's Week* and was described as "sugarland's prettiest, with a skin as clear as sunlight and eyes that sparkled like jewels . . ." It was a comeuppance that should have made her forget the slight, but she would never forget. She came again in December in our last year in college, not to wish us Merry Christmas, but to hand carry an invitation to her wedding. I opened the door and outside was the black Mercedes 220 SE of Senator Reyes with its khaki-uniformed driver. It was such a long time—more than two years—since I had seen her and though I often ached to catch a glimpse of that face, I thought it best to dampen the desire, to let things be. She wore no makeup, her brownish hair shining in the morning sun, her skin glowing. She walked up to me, saying, "Eddie, Eddie—" then she embraced and kissed me—a wet, warm kiss of affection, the scent of her, her hair swirling around me. I was glad to see her and gladder that I was finally as tall as she.

I led her to the house saying inanities while she plied me with questions about school, my career as a sociologist. I asked about her politics, starring in the school musical that was plastered in the society pages, and her singing so well that a bright career was foreseen for her. She waved them all aside, saying she just wanted to be alive, to do nothing if that was possible, and raise a dozen children.

That really brought me back to earth for those children that she would raise would certainly not be mine. Her wedding would be in two weeks.

I had a very good excuse for not going: My major term paper was due and I had to go to my village again to observe the farmers there and see how they were responding to the innovations in rural credit. So I was away when she got married in the Forbes Park church but there were pictures all over, including one in which she was being carried by Lopito over the threshold of the new house that Senator Reyes had built for them.

My sisters where pleased to go; it was their first "society" wedding. Mother and Father were also there, perhaps Narita's "closest relatives." Their presence was imperative for it was Mother who was the *madrina* and I ascribed that to Narita's innate good sense. She was now my "sister" and I often laughed at how ridiculous it seemed afterwards.

By the time I finished college, I met a junior in the Department of Anthropology, a charming Cebuana with a slim figure and a cheerful disposition and, with her, it was easy to forget Narita. After graduation, too, I had a graduate assistantship in the department and before the end of the year, a scholarship to Harvard. I grabbed it although it meant some financial difficulty for my father who still had three other children to send to college.

I did not see Narita again for about three years until I started working for my doctorate. For these lapses in the story, I relied on interviews, on remembered bits of conversation, on clippings of that period but mostly on her, for I never hesitated to ask her the frankest questions.

Tape One

Mrs. Cornelia Cruz, cook:

(I have edited out the questions and repetitions so that this transcript is almost verbatim.)

My name is Cornelia Cruz, widow. I am fifty-eight years old and I was born in Bacolod. I have worked for Senator Reyes and his family for forty years, first as maid then as cook. I am a high school graduate and I learned to cook from Mrs. Reyes who also sent me to study at the Cordon Bleu school every afternoon for six months. I can prepare a European-style meal, Chinese, Indian, at least forty dishes and even an llokano *pinakbet* (vegetable stew) if I were asked to. The Señorita's favorite was *pinakbet*, with lots of prawns in it, instead of pork. She also liked half-ripe mangoes with the special sauce I prepare for it. And yes, salted eggs for breakfast, with tomatoes, and fried rice without lard—but with garlic and onions fried before mixing them with the rice. She always liked her meals hot and never cared much for cold cuts, sandwiches, except yogurt. When she went out, and it was possible, she always had a thermos bottle with her for soup, or tea and, of course, she always liked eating at home. She was a good cook herself and that was why I always tried my best. And yes, she knew meats. She could tell whether it was fresh, whether it was the best part of pork or beef. She even told me of the tricks that those women in the market play on their customers.

I was transferred to the new house of Señorito Lopito a

week before they moved in. It was empty then—actually empty, and they lived in the Manila Hotel for two months while Señorita furnished it. She was very meticulous and her decorator was very exasperated, but the Señorita knew what she wanted. It was such a beautiful house and the garden—it was much better than the senator's. But then, from the very beginning, it was not a happy home. They were always quarreling, from the first day they moved into it. Señorita tried, I think, to be a good housewife, seeing to it that the Señorito's meals were ready when he came home, and she never left home without asking his permission. She never went places—I know because I sometimes accompanied her to Christian's—her dress shop in Malate, to the supermarket, or to parties with former college friends. And of course, the driver always took her there. Señorito always asked him to report where she went. Me, I had to tell him who called at the house, what she said. He was not the best husband, that I can say. But he never beat her although he could have done it for Seriorito easily got violent. All his sports had something to do with violence and death—archery, shooting, fencing. Sei;orita Narita knew how to handle him, I suppose, for though she seldom raised her voice, from their silences, I knew that there was a lot of quarreling going on. Sometimes late in the night, I would hear them arguing. And, you know, our quarters are separate from the house but still I could hear. But then, when there was a party, it was as if she was the happiest girl in the world. And parties, we had them almost every day. I was never so tired and never before had I worked so hard as when I was in that house; but it was also good for I was able to apply what I learned. The Señorito was meticulous. He ordered the flowers, supervised the seating arrangements. I think he was showing off his wife all the time and he was really proud of her—brilliant, a good singer, a good actress—she was everything a man would be proud to marry or possess. Yes, I think it was that way—the Señorito wanted to possess her as if she were some property which, of course, the Señorita was not. She had a mind of her own and a very good mind, too. Sometimes, when I heard them talking, it was she who had a head on her shoulders. The Seriorito would just sit quietly while his wife lectured to him. He really loved her. He bought her clothes and always tried to select materials for them. He bought her jewels, too, lots of them, and whenever they went to Hong Kong, you can be sure they always returned with something very expensive. And paintings, the Señorita introduced them to him, and *santos* and prints; they bought so many there is one room full of them for there is no place to hang them. And antiques, too—well, you see so many shops now selling them but when they started collecting, there was not a single shop where you could really get them. But Señorita Narita had a way and soon other—collectors were coming to the house, showing her things. She had taste, that is what Lopito always said and he felt very proud because he thought it was he who developed her taste. But that is not true; with her, taste was instinctive.

She was also clever. She convinced her father-in-law—that old, scheming man—to divide his property before he died so that there would be no squabbling among his children. And there were only three of them left, you know, so you can imagine how happy the Señorito was to have money of his own, lots of it. But wait, knowing how much of a spendthrift Lopito was, the Old Man saw to it that he could not spend the money without the approval of his wife or of the Old Man himself. And the Señorita—she was always visiting the senator, bringing him cakes which she baked, calling him up, inquiring about his health. And it was all very sincere so that even after they had separated, she continued seeing him and regarding him as a dutiful daughter should. It was a miracle, really, how the marriage could have lasted five years. Five years! It should not have lasted more than a year but that just shows you how patient she was, how she made herself the martyr which she was and this many people do not know. It was all his fault—that I can assure you. From the very beginning. I once heard Señorita telling him, and these were her exact words—"You are not only a liar, you are a coward. You should have told me, from the start . . ." To which Lopito screamed, for he was drunk that night, "So you would have gone out and gotten yourself a dozen men." And the Señorita said, "Not while I am married to you, Lopito. Not while I am your wife. But I will do that the moment I leave this house." I am not too sure about what he was lying about. Or being a coward for. But you must have noticed, there was something effeminate about him. It really started when the Señorito began bringing those boys to the house. Some of them riff-raff, you know. The first time it happened, the Señorita transferred to the second floor guest room. They were sleeping separately in the second year of their marriage and in the third, they were hardly talking; the Señorito still held parties as if nothing had happened. He tried to win her back but it was impossible. Those boys, you know. Then they had this big quarrel, right after a party, for Lopito was flirting with one of the male guests and the Señorita was so embarrassed. That was when she left him—she went to live with her father-in-law. He followed her there and the senator did not know a thing about the boys, you know, and that was when he disowned his son. The Señorita refused to go back to Forbes Park and he really must have missed her, loved her in his own way. Well, you know, he collected guns. It was a shotgun which he used, stuck it into his mouth. It was no accident the way it was made to appear in the newspapers. When he died, the Señorita returned to Forbes Park and redecorated the house, changed everything, sold all the things that belonged to Lopito so that there would be no trace of him: There were less parties—maybe just once a month and I really looked forward to them for by then, I had become a very good cook. Why, I could apply anytime at any of the hotels or first-class restaurants. I have polished my French cooking so much, we had a guest once from Paris and he said he thought it was a French chef who prepared the meal.

END OF TAPE

I had been thorough in the interviews, of which I conducted literally more than a hundred, and I also visited and revisited the places where Narita had been and which were relevant to this story. I was always welcome in the Forbes Park residence and her two boys called me Tito. I knew their housekeeper, a distant aunt from back home in Santa Ana. It is a Spanish-type house, whitewashed, with a red-tile roof and ornately grilled windows. Tiles all over the place, in the balcony, the kitchen, and the trees planted there—the guava and the pomelo are now bearing fruit. Narita never seemed to have forgotten the old house in Santa Ana. And yes, the cadena de amor scrambles over the walls, not too profusely or wildly.

I had often mused about how it must feel to have someone commit suicide over you. I remember distinctly that afternoon we were having coffee in her library and she reminisced about her marriage to Lopito. I had just finished her major speech on the restructuring of Filipino cultural values and we were as a matter of fact, engaged in a discussion on the subject which had fascinated us in the think tank as well. She could have written it herself but, like me, she had taken up too many chores. By then, she had wanted me to leave the university so that I could be on her staff full-time, but I was never sold on politics as a career and, in hindsight, I was, of course, right.

She was in comfortable jeans, denim jacket, her hair in a ponytail. She was the mother of two but she could have easily been one of the juniors on the campus. She was holding a glass of Campari and soda which she herself had mixed and she had given me a glass of Southern Comfort, an affectation I had picked up in Cambridge. We had the house all to ourselves; the maids were asleep in their quarters, and the boys were vacationing with their grandfather in Baguio. She asked me why, at the very old age of thirty-four—which she also was—I had not yet gotten married.

"I suppose I have always been in love with you," I said, at which she laughed aloud, that kind of joking, insinuating laughter which meant that while she appreciated the thought, she also automatically rejected it. She was already one of the most popular women in the country and vastly wealthy, the extent of which I had only started to realize.

"Well, at least you are not a homo," she said, merriment in her eyes. Then it came—sudden, precise, and without any warning. "That was what Lopito was—oh, everyone knew it. Didn't you?"

I nodded.

"He was what you call AC/DC, " she said, her face all seriousness now. "We had such fun in the beginning when he was going to Santa Ana—remember? And here in Manila, too, when he was parading me around. I was good camouflage for him. But I think that in his own way, he sincerely loved me." She paused. Her eyes had misted. "He was so kind, so good to me. He did all that I wanted and I promised myself that I would really be true to him, be an old-fashioned Filipino wife. Do you still see the likes of her?"

"Are you asking me as a sociologist?"

"Yes," she said.

"The society is changing, Narita. Look at you and you understand how times have changed."

She nodded. "It was not the boys that Lopito brought home," she said, "although that aggravated it. It was not his putting me on a pedestal to show off to his friends, to his society crowd. I liked that. I had more beauty, more brains than any of them. " Then it all came through again how the girls at Assumption had snubbed her because she had such lowly origins.

"Lopito, we could have been just friends, you know. As two people can be very good friends, the way we are . . ." She leaned over and pinched me on the thigh. It was more of a caress and it sent delightful shivers through me. "But after we had gotten married, that was when we really had body contact, you know, the kissing and the petting. Man-wife relations. But that was all there was to it. I would be all heated up and anxious and ready—and he could not do it. He could not do it!" She was pounding the throw pillow viciously, her face wrought up in anger, her eyes blazing. I had never seen Narita in such a mood before and I was shocked and frightened.

After Lopito's death, Narita went into mourning, wore the black dress of widows and—as an informant told me of this period—she was if anything more chic in her black dresses. But her grief was real. You cannot live with a person for five years and not have the slightest attachment to him. She retained her married name and preferred to be addressed as Mrs. Reyes even when she went into politics. And her children, too, though they were not Lopito's—she gave them her husband's name. Senator Reyes knew this and it is perhaps for this reason why the Old Man is happy with her children, too.

What would a young, beautiful widow in the Philippines do if she had brains and money as well? The world is wide open and it was at this point that Colonel Antonio Cunio came in. But first, may I point out one basic problem that I also encountered when I started this study.

I had wanted to do a survey of women in politics and we have many examples that date back to the earliest days of suffrage or, if you will, to the revolution against Spain when our women played a vital role. But by zeroing in on a particular subject, a woman I knew very well, I could detail the personal incidents, pry into motivation—all of which cannot be quantified, but which are important in any study. This would, probably, be termed as psychohistory or psychosociology. But I am not one to bother the general reader with obtuse jargon that is often the mumbo jumbo of muddled thinking or which is simply bad writing.

At first, Colonel Cunio, who is now retired, did not want to talk. I had to rely on the usual tricks of the interviewer to thaw out his reserve. I told him that I need not mention his name in the study but afterwards, he gave me blanket authority to use all the "facts" with his name if I wanted to.

As it turned out, he was loquacious, proud of his Korean War record, proud of his machismo.

All that he described happened during the time I was at Cambridge. I had not seen Narita since I left for the United States although in my third year there, I learned that she was in New York. Colonel Cunio was a Philippine Military Academy graduate; he prided himself on his knowledge of Philippine politics and grudgingly admitted that Narita was bright, particularly when she analyzed the Far East. "I don't know where she got that smattering of Japanese," he said wryly, "but when she started talking about periods in Japanese history, and Korea, too, she really had the field to herself."

Tape Two

Colonel Antonio Cunio, retired:

I got my commission in 1947 and that same year, I commanded a platoon in the Huk campaign in Central Luzon. I was a junior at the PMA during the war and could have gotten my commission in the field . . . Nothing spectacular about World War II; we were disbanded in Cagayan and there was some guerrilla work. I was in several operations, including Four Roses—that was when William Pomeroy, the American communist, was captured. I also saw action in the Korean War, I suppose you have read about that although you may have been quite young then. Our battalion figured in the Imjin campaign and that was where I got this Distinguished Service medal. Well, actually, it was a retreat, for the Chinese were coming at us wave after wave and I led a company through a pincer movement. We lost five in that encounter, but I can assure you the Chinese lost many more. They were so close, we were fighting with fixed bayonets. We did no hand-to-hand fighting, but we were lobbing grenades. The barrels of the automatic rifles were hot and still they came, blowing their bugles. I had a flesh wound in the thigh—I did not even know it till one of the men pointed to my bleeding leg and they bandaged it to stop the flow. I was weak but you can rely on this old Tagalog blood to carry me through.

After the Korean War, I was sent to command schools in the United States and that was where I had my first white woman. It was quite an experience, you know. She was the wife of a lieutenant who was assigned to Germany and while she was waiting for her transfer, she came around and provided me company. There was this Korean girl, too, in Pusan. But you know how war is, how things come and go. When I returned after a year at Fort Benning and Fort Leavenworth,

I was assigned to Camp Murphy—called Camp Aguinaldo now—to a desk job that had me bored as all desk jobs do. So I started looking around for patronage—you know, the old Filipino standby. And that was when I saw Senator Reyes who had known my father when my father was still active in Bulacan politics. It was the senator who got me as his aide and, later, when he became Senate President—one step to the Presidency—you know what that means! It was as an aide that I met Narita. I used to deliver messages from the Old Man to her, carry parcels, her blasted cakes, the special gifts that she bought for him when she went abroad, those Dutch cigars in special tinfoil. She was always hanging around the Old Man, attending to him more than his daughters ever did, and Senator Reyes was really eating off her palm. Yes, I think the senator became some sort of father to her. And what a father he turned out to be—more generous than any father would be. And I don't blame him—the way his own children had been treating him as if he did not exist or that he existed only to give them money. I was drawn to her from the beginning, I suppose, although I am ten years older or more. But there is nothing like a younger woman for a middle-aged man. Good and tight, you know what I mean. Then her husband died. It was then that I felt I was free to attend to her. But not before. I still have some sense of ethics left, even when it came to sex. Besides, what would the Old Man say if he found out that I was shacking up with his daughter-in-law? I first dated her a full month after the death of Lopito. She was not a hypocrite. When I asked her if I could take her out nightclubbing at the Amihan, she said yes outright. I told her that it was not one of those high-class places, the food was awful, there were hostesses and she might feel insulted. But I knew she loved good music and there was an excellent band playing there. And she said, yes, don't lecture me about what is decent and indecent; I can decide that for myself. We went in her Mercedes; she said it was better that way because she felt more independent. Damn it—that was what was wrong with her. She always wanted to be independent. To feel independent. To act independent. She did not give much of a chance for even a man like me to be her master. Or at least be on top. Do you know that even when we were doing it, she wanted to be on top? Well, I couldn't do much about that. After all, I really needed her and loved her. I tried to keep it a secret but was not successful. My wife, who is also a very clever woman, got to know of it. But there was my career and I was close to one of the most powerful men in the country. She tried to accept it and keep quiet. Narita, too, wanted to keep up appearances and in a way, she was a very moral person. And that was when she thought she should go to the United States so she could be freer and less inhibited than she was in Manila. The Old Man was also very glad to have her go, to improve herself. And he knew of the relationship—he saw to it that I got an assignment in New York as attaché to the Mission there. I really enjoyed New York—that one year of freedom from the duties in Manila. Narita bought this apartment—or house, rather, in the East Sixties. Ah, you know about it. It cost a fortune then and it certainly must be a very expensive piece of property now. I hope that the radiator in her bedroom is already fixed. It was always squeaking, you know, and was often a bother. You know what I mean. Well, we had a son—her older boy, you know that. And I will never forgive her for giving him Lopito's name. Everyone knew he was not Lopito's. He was mine. And she told the boy it was Lopito who was his father. Not me. I cannot even visit him or tell him he is mine. That woman—she thought of everything. It could be blackmail, of course. But what could I do? I am a government servant and her father-in-law is one of the most powerful men in government. You know what I mean.

And then, she met Ambassador Iturralde. That was my mistake—I introduced her to him at one of those receptions where I thought I would show her off. You know, in any crowd, she would stand out. But you know something? I had one over all of them, over all of the men that she went with afterwards. Yes, no one can get this distinction from me. And I am very proud. It happened finally on our second date. I did not take advantage of her on the first. Just dancing, cheek to cheek, and a simple good-night kiss. Although I knew that she was waiting for me to make the move, I did not want to play it fast. Experience has taught me never to rush, just play it cool and slow. A week afterwards, I asked her if she wanted to go that Sunday for a drive to Bulacan where I grew up. There was this special restaurant along the highway which served wonderful crabs and snipes when they were in season. And she said yes. Of course, I had already made plans on how to seduce her—if seduction is the word. It is all very clear to me, the first time with her, and it was unforgettable, I suppose, also for her. It was a bright Sunday morning and we drove off towards Calumpit and had lunch at this roadside restaurant. She was game. It was not a fancy place and she seemed to enjoy it. Then I asked her if she wanted to see the fish ponds where the crabs and the milkfish were caught, and have a breath of fresh air besides and she said, yes. So we drove off towards the bay where my family had owned this fish pond for years. You pass this village before reaching it—and the villagers worked for my family, you know, and they knew why I was there. I suppose Narita also suspected. We got off at the village and I pointed out to her the ponds that lay beyond the clump of acacia trees at the turn of the river and said, those are ours. There was this hut alone in the expanse of dikes and water where the workers rest and I asked her if she wanted to go out there and take a closer look and she said, of course, and so we went. We were finally there, alone by ourselves. I took her inside the hut and kissed her. She responded with a passion that surprised me, considering that it was the first time I had really kissed her. At first, she was a bit apprehensive when I started taking off her dress, but I said I would keep watch, and that no one from the village would dare come and interrupt us. After all, this was not the first time I had taken a girl to the hut. Assured thus, she gave herself to me with an abandon that was almost anger. I know—and you know something? Damn it—goddamn it! I was the first. The first! All those years that she was married to Lopito, nothing had happened. I have the proof, damn it. I kept it. She was looking around for some tissue paper, but there was none and I had this white, spotless handkerchief which she used. It was all red, all red! I tell you, that is something no one can take away from me!

END OF TAPE

TWO

In the summer of '62, I got a note from Narita; I was in my last year and was deep in work, writing my dissertation, and could not be disturbed, so I merely wrote to her saying thank you, yes, I had heard she was in New York and would visit her very soon, perhaps in early fall. It had been very difficult, living in Cambridge and trying to make my scholarship go farther. But I was fortunate to have a cheap studio off Memorial Drive and within walking distance to the Square. It was on the ground floor of a two-storey wooden frame house with a shingle roof. My landlord—a retired air force sergeant—worked as a security guard at Filene's. His Filipino acquaintances when he was stationed for four years in Clark were black marketeers and hostesses along the Angeles strip and he was pleased to know someone different. He and his termagant wife often did nice things for me—invited me upstairs to dinner or sent me a piece of cake. I had my own entrance from the alley which gave me privacy, but in the winter I had to shovel tons of snow which were dumped on it.

I found it a bit incongruous that I should be working on the rural problems and the family structure of the Philippines in New England when I should have been doing something more original and creative like studying the blacks or even the simpler case of old-timers in Hawaii and the West Coast who were never assimilated into the American mainstream. Filipinos working for their Ph.D.'s in America should study America—otherwise there is no sense in going there, just as Americans working on their Ph.D.'s come to the Philippines for their fieldwork. But there is always a special aura to having an American Ph.D. and we must pay for that aura.

I was very much surprised one afternoon when Narita appeared at my boardinghouse. She was big with child but even though bloated, she looked lovely.

"Eddie, you snob," she said the moment she came in. I glanced at the big car, a Continental, that was parked in the street and inside was an aging *mestizo* whom I recognized at once. He had a Filipino driver up front.

"Isn't that the ambassador?"

"Yes, darling," she said, taking my hand and taking me inside my cluttered room.

"Well, ask him in. I don't mind . . ."

"No, darling," she said sweetly. "Let him wait. After all, I just asked him for a lift so that I could see you."

"All the way from New York?"

She smiled and closed the door behind her.

I had known of Lopito's death two or three years before. Looking at her big belly, I said, "That's progress. So you got married again."

"Ummmm."

"I would like to meet him. Is he in New York with you?"

She tweaked my nose. "You poor dear—so behind the gossip. This is my second. And the father—well, it's that poor man outside waiting for us to finish our small talk."

"You mean the ambassador?"

"Darling, certainly not the driver! Didn't you know?"

I shook my head. She took everything with amusement. "And tell me, how is your dissertation coming along? The other evening, your adviser was in New York, in my house for dinner. Did you know that? I've met a few people. I have dated quite a few interesting men. A certain John F. Kennedy—"

"Really now," I said. Narita was never a braggart. She was just stating a fact.

"Well, it is a long way from Santa Ana, isn't it?" she said. She asked me about my sisters and my parents, how the old town was. She had not been there since her marriage to Lopito but she had dispatched an engineer to build a house, right where the old house stood, so that her mother would have something better to live in.

Long after she left, I wondered what on earth she had come to see me for. I decided to take up her invitation and that December, shortly before Christmas, I went to visit her.

It had already begun to snow in Boston, the last golden leaf of maple had fallen, and a bleakness was all over the landscape. It was an unusually warm December afternoon when I got to the Greyhound bus station on Forty-second Street and because I just had a small weekender suitcase, I decided to walk to her house on Sixty-eighth Street. It was a good, invigorating walk up Fifth Avenue with its Christmas decor, the smell of roasting chestnuts in the air. I paused briefly at the Rockefeller Plaza where ice skaters were showing off.

Her house was in a residential area on the East Side, a short walk from Central Park, a neighborhood of walk-ups and boutiques. She was expecting me, and she answered the doorbell. Narita, I saw again, was beautiful, her hair falling down her shoulders, her lips red though without a touch of lipstick. She embraced me warmly and gave me another of those full, wet kisses. She smelled of cologne and freshness and all the wonderful scents I remembered of her. She was slim again and she said, "Yes, I had a boy. I have two boys now. Want to see them?"

She took me to the basement which was prettied up into a nursery. I noticed at once that the older boy was dark and the newborn was, like her and Iturralde, very fair.

She smiled at me, divining my thoughts, and pinched me on the side. "I will tell you everything," she said.

The house had four storeys including the basement. The ground floor opened to a narrow garden which she had done with rocks, evergreens and huge clam shells from the Philippines. A wisteria filled the other end. I could imagine how beautiful it would be all lighted up for some evening party. Nothing ostentatious about the house although the furnishings were expensive, the beige leather sofas, the Afghan rugs, the soft blue velvet drapes. She had an Albers, two Pollocks, plus her paintings from the Philippines, *santos,* and antique china which would cost a fortune in New York as they already did in Manila. She had three full-time Filipino maids, one a registered nurse who looked after the babies and the house. They occupied two of the rooms in the basement and had their own entrance.

Narita had prepared *pinakbet* which I was not particularly fond of, but the fact that she had cooked it herself, touched me. She ate a little for she would be going out that evening to a dinner. She would miss the cocktails but since it was close by, she would have more time with me. I wanted to ask many questions but I didn't have to; she was telling me many things and at the same time asking me about Santa Ana.

"I am not going to be his mistress forever, " she said finally. "His wife won't divorce him. But even if she did, I won't marry him. He is a wonderful, thoughtful man—and he has given me all the love and attention that someone in his position can give. He is also a very lonely man, a very misunderstood man, and I love him very much. "

"What is love to you now, Narita?"

I had not meant the question to be so crude.

She was holding the silver spoon and had just ladled out another spoonful of the vegetable stew into my plate. We were in her dining room, before that finely carved rosewood table with the silver candelabra and its four unlighted candles and lace tablecloth.

I had already taken off my jacket and was very comfortable in my turtleneck sweater. I had even shucked off my shoes and had really made myself at home.

"Do not ask me to make definitions," she said sharply. "Look at me, what I do, how I react. What are words?"

"Extensions of our thoughts."

"But they could be different from what we do. And I want to do a lot, to live a lot. I also know where I am headed. I have two boys—but that's not enough. I could live for them, but what do we live for anyway? You ask me what love is, you may just as well ask why I am alive . . ."

I had not intended to get into a philosophical discussion only to get lost in a maze of contradictions, but she was doing the talking. "We all grow up," she said. "Or am I presuming things?"

I held her hand.

"Did you know that I have an M.A. in Far Eastern studies from Columbia?"

I had heard about her studying, but the degree surprised me—not that she did not have the talent for it but that she had the perseverance.

"It is always fun, trying to learn more." She spoke humbly. Then, "But some men—all they want out of life really is sex, and after that is over, you have to talk a bit, right?"

I smiled in agreement.

"I have had my fill of that type. In fact, one of them is the father of my older boy. You looked surprised when you saw him . . . He was an aide of Papa," she explained simply. "He was a military type, you know, chest out, chin in, all muscle and no brain. Oh, it was a wonderful, physical relationship, all the orgasms that I had read about but never knew till I met him. But he was a stud—nothing more, just a stud, and how boring he could get after he was used!"

No woman had ever spoken to me before as frankly as she did, and for the first time, I felt uneasy with her and something akin to apprehension. But it went away quickly for she laughed then and asked about my latest girlfriend.

I was dating a Radcliffe girl at the time, a sweet Southerner from Memphis who often came to my place to bake corn bread and cook that slightly hot Southern dish with lots of okra, prawns and tomatoes in it, it almost tasted Filipino. I described Anne, her vices and her virtues, but not our lovemaking.

It was just five o'clock but already it was dark and she got up and switched on the lamps. There was no doubt in my mind that I desired her. In my younger days, I often fantasized about how she would look in the nude. I remembered those times when we were ten or eleven and we raced in the rain and bathed in the creek beyond their house. Her breasts were just beginning to shape and her nipples, small pinkish dots showed beneath her cotton chemise as she rose. from the water.

I had finished a plateful of California rice and some of the vegetable stew. She stood up to put away the dishes for the maid to wash in the morning. In a minute, she called from the kitchen. "So, how often do you have it now that Anne has gone home for the holidays?"

"I can be a celibate till she returns," I said. "And how about you? You said he won't be back in Washingon till February."

She returned and led me to the sofa in the living room. "It's no problem," she said, laughing.

"Without Anne, it is a problem," I said. "You have to spend a bit on a girl, take her out to dinner, buy her some candy—all those preliminaries that most American girls seem unable to do without."

"I have dildos," she said.

"Isn't that rather boring and automatic?"

Again, that tinkling laughter. "Not if they are live ones."

Then she looked at me with that kind of knowing, inquiring look I couldn't mistake.

"I am no dildo, Narita," I said.

She pressed close to me. "I know," she said, rising; she took me down the corridor to her room. "We will take a bath together," she said matter-of-factly.

I marveled at the clearness of her skin, as she let me look at her, her breasts, still firm though she had two boys, the flat stomach, unusually unmarked by childbirth. "You must be careful now," she said, "or else I may have to go back to the hospital. After all, it's only been a month—and this is the first . . ."

I was only half-listening; I was too engrossed with her beauty. She was telling me that men never had a sense of responsibility—it was the women all the time who had to be responsible, but that was fully taken care of now. She told the doctor who delivered her baby that she did not want another, ever, and the doctor had seen to that.

I would have been creation's most exultant being and there was no hardship I would not have dared; but in that moment when I thought earth and high heaven were finally mine, she pushed me, not brusquely, but certainly with enough force to let me know, to remind me that I should be careful and in that businesslike voice that was a chill change from her caress, she said, "You are messing my hair, Eddie, and I still have that dinner tonight . . ."

She woke me when she returned a little before midnight and she slipped into bed, cuddling close, her breath smelling a little of wine, her hands wandering all over me. I desired her still but it was her comment about the human dildo that bothered me and would always continue to bother me. I was passive throughout. If she noticed it, she did not say anything. She had her pleasure, more perhaps than the ambassador could give her, and when she was finally tired, she lay beside me.

"I really have no one to talk to here," she said. "The Americans can be very good friends but they seem so superficial and their view of the world is really limited, not so much by their experience but by what the media tells them. They lack intuition, the passion to see things not just as objects, the way we can do it—"

I asked her to put it simply.

"I thought I was explicit," she said. "I'm tired of America. I want to return home. I have been here too long. Papa is getting senile. I'd like to go into politics when I return . . ."

I had to get used to her calling Senator Reyes "Papa."

"You'll botch it all up, " I said. "You have too much candor, too much openness."

"Only with people I really know," she said.

"What does the ambassador say?"

"I will leave him soon—he doesn't know it yet. But that is a sure thing. "

"Just as you left that colonel?"

She pressed my hand and was silent.

"I want you to help me when I go into politics. You don't have to worry about your job in the university. I know that you will command a very high price—but Eddie, I will make it all up to you. On your terms."

"But why me?"

"Because you know me," she said with feeling. "My weaknesses. You will protect me, and you will be loyal to me—just as I will be loyal to you, in my own way."

"But what can I do?"

She was silent again for a while; then she started: "It is really time that we had more brains in our politics, not the old backslapping, vote-buying kind. Magsaysay thought he had all the answers, but actually, he was old-fashioned, buying off the journalists the way he did. No, we can be more scientific than that. If you know what I mean. We should have constant polls, quantify, analyze trends. These are sophisticated approaches. This doesn't mean that we will abandon the old methods—the guns and goons, the bribery, the innuendo and the false rhetoric—the way Papa had done. And the Old Man, you must admit, has gone very far . . ."

"But politics is just an instrument, Narita," I said, annoyed at the brazen implications of what she was saying. "There must be something behind it. Meaning: What is power to you?"

For a while, she did not speak. In the soft light, her face was grim until she broke into a smile. "I will show them," she said. "I will show them . . ."

"Show whom?"

"Those nitwits in Assumption. I was the only girl from Santa Ana. They came from Silay, Bacolod, Iloilo—you know, with their twelve-hectare *haciendas,* acting like princesses. And they had nothing between their dirty ears."

I remembered Father's few hectares from which he made so little, barely enough to pay for the mortgage of the house in Diliman, for our education and I reminded her we had only a few hectares.

"But you never snubbed me, Eddie—not till recently, and I had to go to you on bended knees. I will take care of you, too," she laughed. "In fact, I have already done that." She pressed her warm breasts to me.

"You can't embark on something like this, nursing an old hurt. That was years ago, Narita. You have to live and work beyond it. If you become a congressman . . ."

She drew away. "You must be kidding. I won't start that low. Nothing less than the Senate for me. Let me tell you this: I know much more than all those asses in the Senate, including my father-in-law. Five years in the United States, I know how power works here, in New York, in Washington. I know all the important House and Senate members, the Ways and Means Committee, the Foreign Relations Committee. And their aides—mind you, never forget the aides. Why, the ambassador often relies on me for advice. Do you know what I am trying to say? For as long as we are an American colony, we should know how our colonial masters operate. And, brother, this is where it starts."

Her brief exposition on Washington politics was impressive; she had not gone to Columbia for nothing.

"Do you have a program?" I asked.

"Of course," she said instantly. "Also, one for how to get to power . . ."

I was getting a bit dizzy and I did not want to ask more questions. She just went into a quiet monologue: "On the local level, meaning Negros, I would like to dismantle the sugar industry. It is a colonial industry and it has tied us to the United States. Unless, of course, the quota system is given up."

I wanted to ask her how she could do that, her Papa being in sugar, the ambassador being in Washington for no other reason than to protect our sugar interests. And my family, what would happen to us? We knew nothing except sugar . . .

"I'm interested in culture as well. Not just in the arts, that's common enough. But in reshaping our mores. Sociocultural engineering. You know what I mean. And in foreign affairs, I want our relationship with Japan and China analyzed further, clarified. We should recognize China immediately. I told Jack—"

"Jack who?"

"Kennedy, of course," she said, poking me in the ribs. "When he was a senator—that it was wrong for the United States not to have any relationship with China. China is not a threat to the United States, the way the Soviets are, and Japan will be. Japan is a real threat to us—and our damned politicians and businessmen, they are selling us down the river."

"I hope you will not end up being like them," I said.

"No, Eddie," she said gravely. "For one, I don't need money now. I am rich—very rich. And I need help from young people like you because you are not yet a victim of habit, because you'll be anxious to prove yourself, try out new ideas. And you will be surprised to find how really close we are. And I am not talking about this . . ." She kissed me briefly. "Maybe because we come from the same small place, that's not even on most Philippine maps . . . But don't you ever remind me of it again."

Tape Three

Domingo Guardia, private secretary to Ambassador Iturralde:

I am from La Consolacion. My father had worked for the Iturraldes as accountant and it was the ambassador who sent me to college and I worked for him till the day he died. I am not going to tell you anything which is not known to many people, including Dona Alicia. Anyway, both of them are dead now and what I will say will not hurt anyone, even if you do not live up to your promise of discretion. Out of loyalty, I must insist that you edit my comments carefully and use my name sparingly. Mind you, I am not bound by government regulations. I was never employed full-time by the government. I was always hired as consultant or on a contractual basis. My pay comes from Iturralde and Company. Yes, I remember the ambassador told me when he returned from Manila that he had attended a wedding of the son of Senator Reyes. They were very good friends, you know—sugar and politics. If I am not mistaken, he said something about how beautiful Narita was and it was a shame that she had to marry someone like the son of the senator who was known to be good for nothing. Well, he met Narita again in Washingon about five years later, I think, after her husband died. She just had a baby by that colonel and the ambassador felt strongly about the man—that he was not fit for her. They were not married so he really had no compunctions about having him sent back to Manila so that he could have the field to himself. One thing about the ambassador, he was a very decisive man. He knew what he wanted. I think he explained the situation to Senator Reyes. At least, he didn't want his wires crossed. I wrote some of the delicate communications on the matter, you know, and before the colonel knew it, he was given his walking papers—I mean, he was reassigned to Manila. It was neat and simple. The ambassador was old enough to be Narita's father. She seemed to be attracted to older men. In a way, it was Doña Alicia's fault. She never liked traveling, the cold climate, and in the many years that he was in Washington, she visited him only once—for a month. She would rather stay in La Consolacion, in that old rambling house, tending her orchids or, on occasion, going to Manila to visit friends and dine at the Casino. And since they had no children—she could not have one—it was not so difficult for the ambassador to rationalize the affair. I really don't remember too well how it started but all of a sudden, the ambassador was always in a hurry to go to New York on weekends. Sometimes, he even took the Greyhound. Imagine—Ambassador Iturralde on a bus! I have seen pictures of Narita before, on the cover of Philippine magazines. But you know something? She also appeared in

Town & Country, in *Harper's Bazaar*—and that takes some doing, with no publicity agent. It was her beauty, her wit, her circle of friends and, most of all, her gracious ways that did it. She was truly our first international beauty—and she had enough mixed blood to be fair but enough Malay features as well to be a Filipina. When I first met her at the embassy Christmas party, she was coming down the stairs, holding on to the arm of the ambassador. She was in a black gown, no lipstick, no jewels and God knows she had lots of them, including the diamonds that the ambassador bought for her as a matter of habit. I know because I used to go to Tiffany's to pay for them. I also looked after their insurance, all that sort of thing. She was the prettiest creature I had ever seen, prettier than Miss America or Miss Universe. We all paused to look at her and when she moved into any circle, conversation stopped. We did not want to talk for fear that we would be distracted. We just wanted to look at her, those eyes, those lips, that perfect nose. Oh, I am forgetting myself. I always do when I see a beautiful woman. How lucky can you get—I am speaking of that colonel, of course. He did not deserve her. Well, the ambassador had had several women before Narita; this girl from New York, very good in her own way, but you know how American women are—they are never feminine enough. And there was this Spanish girl, royalty—from Madrid. But these were ordinary affairs. Nothing profound about them the way it was with her. I know. The driver knows. She rarely came to the embassy although the ambassador was always taking her to receptions and dinners and introducing her as Mrs. Reyes. But everyone knew of course. The ambassador seemed revitalized. You know that old Chinese belief. I will tell you—one of her rare visits to Washington—it was Saturday, too, and all the staff was out, except me because I had something to rush. I always worked overtime, you know how private secretaries are. Well, I bade them good-bye but I forgot something and had to return to my room. I had a key, you know, and floors carpeted as they are and me quiet as a cat, they did not know I was back. They had locked the door, but not the door to my room which adjoined the ambassador's reception. There was a big sofa there—and they were doing it right there. I looked and I tell you, the ambassador still had it in him. Don't include this—what does it show? That I am a Peeping Tom? I only wanted to show that she was good for him. They stayed on till close to nine o'clock. I did not bring my coat and it was cold outside and I was hungry. So I went back downstairs and started banging doors and turning on the lights and the ambassador came to my room and I feigned surprise that they were still there, and I said I had forgotten some work and my coat—and, you know, they took me out to dinner before they drove me home. He changed his will twice; I typed them both. When his son was born, he changed it again. He gave her a big slice of his property, a house he had bought shortly after the war, in Washington at the other end of Massachusetts Avenue. It is worth over a million dollars now. And, of course, stocks in the mines, many of the things in his name which won't be questioned in board meetings and all that sort of thing. All those diamonds. And part of that cash at Chase Manhattan and a bank account in Zurich—things that Doña Alicia never knew about and did not care to know. He would have married her—you know, specially after their son was born. He wanted her to use his name but in the end felt it was wiser that her married name be used. What does it matter anyway? After all, no one can deny the boy's parentage. And come to think of it, both her children are American citizens—having been born in the United States. I wish I also had that advantage. I could have applied for it; after all, I had lived there so long and the ambassador would have helped me. But America is not for old people. I really don't know what made her leave him—oh, it is not as tragic as you'd think it was. It was a quiet parting of the ways, with no regrets. After all, she was just returning to the Philippines where he could see her anytime he wanted. And there were also the trips that she made to the United States anytime he asked her to come. But it was a separation just the same. After that, the ambassador drooped. The fires in him died, the juices ran out. He was not the same again. It was really just a matter of time before the cancer finally got him. But he had lots of memories. When he was dying, he would call her up and there would be tears in his eyes. I sometimes listened to the conversation. It would often last for a full hour and he would ask about his boy and Narita would come loud and clear on the line. It was very happy and also very sad.

END OF TAPE

THREE

My adviser in Harvard was a Southeast Asian specialist whose real interest lay in the Philippines and those aspects of what he termed "early American imperialism." Dr. Donald Harten and his wife even spent a sabbatical in a village in Leyte and he spoke enough Waray to get by in a rural setting. He did not want a compilation of empirical data that would be buried in library indexes like most theses in the past. He wanted something which would be useful and he was always posing questions that made me rethink earlier premises so that my initial writing on the changing patterns of rural family behavior, as innovations were introduced to it, was altered into an analysis of the family not just as a rural institution but as the core of society and as power broker. I say all this now remembering how Senator Reyes was the patriarch in our part of the country and how he had drawn to his fold someone like Narita and the husbands of his two daughters who, I later learned, were handpicked by him not for what they were but for what they could contribute to the Reyes dynasty. My dissertation was wide ranging and discursive and I saw much later how some of the concepts that I had developed were operating in the political campaign that I had witnessed.

I was disturbed by an earlier comment Narita had made in New York when I told her about the inevitability of my returning to the state university and "paying back" my scholarship; she had said that the UP was an elitist school just like Ateneo, La Salle, and Assumption; it was not contributing to the socialization of knowledge and I would do some good if I taught instead in any of the diploma mills where the poorer classes went. I have thought a lot about what she had said but I needed, I must admit, the prestige of the UP and, also, I knew that the workload there and the pay were much better than in those sweatshops on Azcarraga.

Returning to Manila after five years in Cambridge was a traumatic experience. First, the heat. It was April when I left the United States and San Francisco where I spent a few days was deliciously cool. So was Honolulu where I stayed with friends at the East West Center and took to the beach at Ala Moana for a week. Then, Manila—and wham! The heat suffused everything, every single pore of the body, and sweat poured out of me like I was a leaking faucet. And the filth! Boston is not America's cleanest city—a friend from Texas said it was Houston—but it was antiseptic compared to what one saw in Manila's main streets, not to mention the back alleys. And the smell—God, the stench of rot, of decay, of brackish *esteros*—it hangs over everything like a dismal monsoon.

In Diliman many new houses had gone up, most of them ostentatious with their ornate doorways and plaster work and our house now looked forlorn and shabby beside them.

I had a ready position at the university as associate professor—that was what a Ph.D. did and though the salary was not much, it was enough. I was filled with the usual coming-home expectations, the resentment towards the old fogies who should be retired to let in young blood, the eagerness to try out new theories and an unabashed lack of humility, I think, that went with the degree. I adjusted fairly quickly.

In the week that I arrived, one of the first people I called up was Narita. I retained fond memories of that weekend in her house and wondered if there would be a repeat. I was not going to push it, though. There were summer classes but I did not have any; I was just in the department fixing up my new desk and the schedule I would have in June.

"I'm on my way out, Eddie," she said. "Can I come and pick you up? We can have dinner together . . ."

I argued against the long drive from Forbes Park but she was adamant. She was not driving, she said.

As luck would have it, by five that afternoon, some of my colleagues had come in and we were all there, bantering and talking shop when she arrived wearing a summer dress and high heels. She rushed over and planted a kiss on my cheek. My colleagues applauded. They gathered around her; they did not even wait for me to introduce her. They started congratulating her for the piece on the Far East in the last issue of the *Sunday Times Magazine.* It was Dr. R. D. Badoc, chairman of the Asian Institute, who was literally gushing over it. "I am glad you said it, Mrs. Reyes," he was saying. "Who else could say that we should recognize Red China now? We would be branded immediately as commies. And your observations about Japan . . ."

"She has an M.A. in Far Eastern studies from Columbia," I said.

"We know," they chorused.

"She speaks Japanese and Mandarin . . ."

The same knowing nods. Then Dr. Badoc asked her: "It is a shame that we cannot afford you. But if you are willing to accept chicken feed, would you like to teach at my Institute?"

"I will consider it," Narita said sweetly. "Let's shake on it," she held out her hand and Dr. Badoc, the perennial woman chaser, held it for some time.

We proceeded to the waiting Mercedes 280 SE, the parade following us. I was walking on a pillow of feathers. We went to Makati—how the place had changed, the soaring new buildings, the wide streets! I thought we would go to the new hotel at one end of the square but we went instead to the supermarket coffee shop and took a table close to the door. We ordered hamburgers and coffee. It was then that I realized what a politician Narita had become. The visit to the university, her meeting my crowd, even the seat we took in the supermarket—all provided her direct contact with people.

When she arrived from the United States, as we had discussed in New York earlier, she should maximize her exposure but be careful in her image building. She had written a paper in school on China's and Japan's relations with Southeast Asia; she had merely halved the article, added some contemporary comments, then walked over to the editor of the largest Sunday magazine in the country. Not only was the article published in two installments, she was also photographed in color for the magazine cover. Now she was all over the society pages. To keep busy in New York, she had written a modern *zarzuela* (musical drama or operetta) on the labor problem—the *sacadas* (migrant workers)—of Negros. Poor boy, rich girl sort of story and maudlin, as most zarzuelas go. That established not just her acting and singing talents but also her concern for social justice. And in an interview on television, she had attacked the American bases and echoed the clichés of her father-in-law. The nationalists lapped it all up. She was asked to do a column for one of the newspapers and she did it with aplomb and easily dethroned Etang Papel who had been considered the finest woman columnist in Manila. All these in less than a year. She had really taken off!

When school opened in June, I was anxious about my classes and eager to make an impact. I wanted sociology to be not just a credit subject; I was determined to make it a window into the society so my students could understand it better, its weaknesses. I was all fired with Relevance. By then, too, I was involved with Narita's career, how I could help shape it. I had no illusions about being a Professor Higgins, for she was no cockney lass. I decided to take down notes of our meetings, the subjects discussed, what courses of action were to be taken. But looking back, there was hardly any new insight that I could glean; all that I did was emphasize the obvious which is, perhaps, the function of the scholar, to dig for bones and then call those bones what they are—bones.

After school had started and routine had settled, she asked me to set up a think tank—not necessarily from my university but from my age group, not just academics but even businessmen and journalists who might be able to contribute something creative to the fossilized political thinking and planning then. There were seven of us—a disparate group which was good, for there is nothing like disagreement to sharpen one's reasoning. I was, of course, the unofficial chairman although we never took votes or suggested one solution to any problem; always, there were options and what would happen if a certain option was picked up. The members:

—Ismael del Mundo, nationalist businessman
—E. Hortenso, Marxist professor of politics
—Julio Acosta, Jesuit historian
—Greg Collantes, novelist
—M. B. Reyes, editor
—Tomas Monte, farm leader

By the end of the year, we had to include a new name in our group. Dr. E. Samonte, statistician. Not one of us was past fifty and it was Dr. Samonte whom everyone called Doctor in deference to his seniority for he was fifty-five. At first, we did not ask for any remuneration; it was enough that we were doing something other than what we were normally engaged in. It was also flattering for us to be asked by Narita, particularly after she had won the election. Now, we considered ourselves closer to the center of power and we could finally do something about the ideas that churned in our minds.

Academicians often have notions about good government, even a commitment to it, but are never given the opportunity to test their ideas or move the awesome and massive machinery. Narita also knew how much professors were paid. In the group, for instance, it was only del Mundo who had a car. Even Dr. Samonte had to ride in jeepneys. But money was of no consequence to Narita and a representation allowance of one thousand pesos each in 1966, even before she won the election, was something.

I have always wanted to know Senator Reyes personally. His speeches had impressed me with their depth and probity and that Sunday evening at Narita's Pobres Park residence, I finally got to meet him. She had sent us an RSVP card, saying it was a sit-down dinner, and I was the first to arrive. I had many questions to ask, the most important of which was how she would be able to reconcile her nationalist platform with her being a member of the sugar bloc; how she would now bring justice to the sugar *sacadas* whose lives she had commented on in her *zarzuela*. She could always retort that I should pose the same questions to the senator. But, at least, Senator Reyes never claimed a social conscience; he was an old cacique who wanted the whole pie and cut off the Americans—a sentiment shared by many politicians turned entrepreneurs.

I now realize that these contradictions did not bother Narita; her concern was not image any longer or the ideological foundation for her campaign, but strategy. And we were her generals.

That was the night I should have quit but I did not have the sense then to dichotomize my vanity, my needs, from the full meaning of integrity. I glowed with self-importance; I was an agent of change, and were it not for the likes of me, the forces of decay, of evil, would triumph. And looking at myself at the time I now realize why the technocrats in government today—for all their objectivity and decency—will never leave the corrupt regime not only because they have power and prestige but because they feel that without themselves in government, it could be worse. That, of course, is their highest form of delusion.

Narita wore black pants and the new style *barong* designed by her dressmaker. She was elegant; and, tonight, instead of kissing me on the cheek, it was on the lips with a little insinuation of her tongue and just as my fancies were starting, she brought me crashing back to earth: "Your deadline for that Muslim profile will be on Monday, Eddie. I know you always meet your deadline, but I am reminding you nonetheless . . ." And with that, she went into chitchat, guiding the conversation where she thought it should go, never wasting my time, always pumping information out of me.

By seven-thirty, everyone was in and the talk became livelier with Royal Salute, Wild Turkey and cognac. Nothing but the best in Narita's house and tonight, even her bartender wore white. It was April and steaming outside, but I should have put on a jacket for the air-conditioning was on full blast and even in that cavernous, living room, it was freezing. We were arguing about centralizing data and Isme del Mundo suggested a computer. It was at this moment that Senator Reyes arrived, saying that he had to leave his poker session although he was already winning a hundred thousand pesos—well, anything for his favorite daughter.

I had not seen him since he came to Santa Ana to address our graduating class and he seemed to have changed but little except for the white mane and the slightly perceptible stoop. He was as dark as the bottom of a pot and his pugnacious face which was familiar to all of us in Negros was rendered malevolent by his eyes which were narrow slits, the pouches bulging from under them. Narita brought him in and we stood up as he slouched on the sofa before us. "We were talking about a computer, Papa, which we need for the campaign and for other things. You can feed it all that mess in your office and simplify your operation as well . . ."

"Order it tomorrow, *hija*," he said indulgently, taking the glass of cognac that the waiter immediately handed him.

Del Mundo, always conscious of costs and particular with figures, spoke then: "It is very expensive, Senator. At least a quarter of a million dollars and we would have to train programmers and a staff to run—"

The Old Man did not even look at Isme. "You can raid any of the companies in Manila that have the competent people, *hijo*. Make that your job, offer them incentives. IBM should be able to satisfy us. And as for taxes . . ." He did not continue; he was not president of the Senate for nothing.

At dinner, it was all trivia interspersed with the senator's bawdy jokes which were pathetically dated. Narita did not laugh at them and, at first, I thought she was being prudish as we, ourselves, hypocrites, were laughing as if we had not heard them before. The Old Man was sharp. "Narita does not laugh at these jokes anymore," he said dryly. "She has heard them so many times but she lets me tell them just the same."

It was a fine French meal that started with vichyssoise. With our stomachs finally stuffed with soufflé, cups of coffee in hand, we proceeded to the library for the session that was to last till four in the morning, the senator lording over it. He started with gandiloquence and self-depreciation:

"Politics is the highest form of human enterprise for with politics, we shape the state and, therefore, the nature of society. It is an honorable profession made dishonorable by rascals like myself who have, like bad weeds, lived this long. I must go but the state lives on. And if you want to better the state, then look at politicians as necessary evils. Not that Narita is evil—," he looked at his daughter-in-law seated on the arm of the sofa, her hand on his shoulder. "But she is a pretty little devil, isn't she?" We all laughed and Narita accepted the compliment with a smile. She really had the Old Man wrapped around her little finger and I wouldn't have been surprised then if the senator, the old goat that we all knew him to be, desired her, too. Then, "I have discussed it with the President and all the Party chieftains. I could have made a unilateral decision, but I believe in the democratic process. And, besides, this will be the first time that the Party will have a beautiful and brilliant candidate."

The king is dead! Long live the king! We all clapped in complete harmony. Now, we really had work to do, now we had an objective—to win the election—two years away.

"You are all family now," the senator boomed. "So let us talk frankly. Candidly. You are also *novatos*—but brilliant *novatos* who have ideas. Or is it plots? I would like to hear all of them. Talk of nothing else but how to win . . ."

The discussion was freewheeling; we started with regional issues, the Ilocos and tobacco and the possibility of reestablishing the cotton industry there. Tourism for the Mountain Province and resettlement in Cagayan Valley and in the foothills of Sierra Madre. Rice and agarian reform in Central Luzon. Decentralization of the sugar industry, fishing in the Visayas and intensified agriculture, the Muslim problem in Mindanao. Then we went into foreign relations, the American bases and, finally, tactics.

Narita participated in this discussion but all talk stopped whenever the Old Man made a point or suggested details. He had, after all, four decades of practice. He was right. We were novices and we never talked about cheating, the use of violence, intimidation, pork-barrel funds, and blackmail; these were real instruments, but we blithely ignored them.

Narita and the Old Man were peeved. I had not known how very much alike they had become in their thinking. "If it will mean victory, then cheat!" the Old Man pontificated.

"The objective is to win," Narita said coolly. "You cannot talk morality with opponents who are immoral. You cannot tell the truth to people who will not accept that truth."

I felt uneasy; my training was different. In that small town where I was born, my parents had pounded a little bit of honesty into me.

"You must always have options," Narita was continuing. "That is what politics is. Always the possible . . ."

We were exhausted although the fruit, cake, coffee, and liquor came continuously. Saliva dripped from the corner of the Old Man's mouth and Narita dutifully wiped it off. He was starting to doze off, and she told him to go upstairs and sleep but he said he would go home. We took him to his car and bade him good-night. The others were driven home but I stayed behind.

Alone, finally, she cuddled close as we talked, the stereo playing Chopin softly. She sighed. "I can hardly wait to put everything into motion, Eddie. I know you have reservations, but, for my sake, don't remind me of that small house—not in the presence of others. The past is just for the two of us . . ."

"I did not talk about Santa Ana," I said.

"You did, too."

"No."

"Want to bet?" She went to the desk at the other end of

the library, fiddled with some knobs in a drawer. The music stopped and clearly, very clearly, our voices—excited and pitched—came alive. She had taped the entire discussion; the library, perhaps the whole house, was bugged.

The pre-convention plan was set. Her *zarzuela* was transported to Davao, Dumaguete, Bacolod, Cebu, Iloilo, and even Dagupan. It was bringing culture to the provinces. She was also invited to lecture at the universities in the South, all the way to a small college in Bongao, Sulu, and there was her thrice-a-week column that I liked to read for its freshness and unpredictability.

In the process, she was making political profiles of the provinces and checking up with the senator on the personalities she had met or wanted to meet.

She learned fast and she had a retentive memory. When the computer came at the end of the year, I wondered how necessary it really was. She had committed to memory so many things, she could have won without it.

FOUR

I have seen Narita in tears only once. By this time, she already had a suite in her father-in-law's Makati building, the nerve center for her political future. She had an excellent clipping service. She had called me, I thought, about some urgent problem. When I arrived, she closed the door, told me to sit down and read an item in a weekly gossip column by Mita Guzman.

Narita never had much respect for Filipino journalists—an attitude she got from Senator Reyes who handed envelopes at the end of every month to a wide assortment of reporters. They covered the Senate and other trivia and passed themselves off as journalists. She had the long list and on it were editors, some of whom professed the highest moral motives.

Mita Guzman was a slight acquaintance; so was the husband, a small, henpecked man who was once my classmate in political science but who had dropped out to take a job as PR man for one of the congessmen. She was a woman to be feared both physically and otherwise for she had the face and the muscle of a sumo wrestler and the nastiness to skewer anything that crossed her path. Now, in her column: "She is young, pretty, and able. She has a Columbia degree and she sings well in a modern musical. Watch out for this girl now for though her father died a drunk and her mother sold meat (not rotten) in the old hometown, she has claims to royalty and will yet make it to the Senate next election . . ."

When I finished the item, which was encircled in red, Narita said: "Why can't they forget where I came from? Did I commit a crime? We were poor, Eddie, but not starving. You know that . . ."

I went to her and held her shoulders. "You should expect these things. Remember, Narita, you're in politics now. There will be more when you campaign. It will not stop."

"I will get her, I tell you," she said grimly, then quavered and tears ran from her eyes. I held her close and could feel her heart thrashing. She clung to me as if I were a raft and cried, the sobs stifled. I did not know whether it was in anger or grief. I said: "There is nothing to be ashamed of, Narita. How many Filipinos are poor? This is your capital, if you want to make it work for you. Cinderella story. Girl from the sticks makes it in New York. Is there a more romantic theme?"

She stopped crying abruptly and drew away, a look of surprise, of resentment, on her tear-washed face. "What?" her voice leaped. "Expose myself to more ridicule? That's unthinkable! I'll have none of it. Poverty is not something to be proud of. It is degrading and don't ask me to think otherwise."

She did get Mita Guzman, in her own way. One morning I came upon Guzman waiting in Narita's Forbes Park living room, a bunch of red roses in her hand. When Narita came out, she attended to me first as if Mita did not exist. And only after she had put Mita in place did Narita go to her, kiss her on the cheek, and thank her for the flowers. Mita waited outside while Narita and I had coffee leisurely in the kitchen where she told me how she did it.

The Guzmans had hocked their house to the Philippine Bank to buy a small press. Having learned of this, Narita—through the Senate President—turned the screws and Mita had no alternative but to come a-visiting. Mita had been to see her more than a dozen times, enriching some florist with the roses she always brought.

To complete the noose, Narita suggested that with her help, the Guzmans should have a larger press capability and they should not worry about printing jobs. There was so much in the Senate that they could do. And then, there was this election campaign that was coming. And yes, she was such a good writer, it would be great if she did Narita's official biogaphy—and of course, Narita would pay for it all and reward their publishing company handsomely.

"She is also cuckolding her husband, " Narita said. "It's all in the computer now. She is no different . . . the whole bunch . . ."

I wanted to say that her father-in-law and she made them that way, but by then, I had decided to keep such thoughts to myself.

If the Party convention was *lutong makaw* (prearranged), so was the election. I watched the campaign and sometimes helped distribute those envelopes with money in them. She had exhausted most of us just keeping up with her. I don't know where her iron energy came from—it certainly was not the yogurt, nor the pills. She would be up mapping out the next meeting with her flip cards and notebooks while we were still asleep. I would have recorded more of her techniques and performance but my leave from the department was up.

She had all the handbills that she needed but there was one picture-poster of her, printed in Japan through the courtesy of Senator Reyes' Japanese contacts, a big 16" × 24" in full color, a prim, almost Mona Lisa-like smile on her face, so elfin, yet so innocent like the Virgin Mary's as well. There was no name on the picture but in those few months, it had become the most popular election material. She autographed it and it was displayed—just like a magazine cover—

which it had been earlier for all the vernacular weekly magazines whose editors she had bought. I saw it inside *sari-sari* stores, in farm homes, in offices long after the campaign and I presume that to this day, there are rural houses adorned with it.

Those flip cards really helped. Before she went into a new territory, the team zeroed in on it, the important people, personal details—hobbies, deaths, birthdays, relatives—all these came in handy. She did not upstage the other candidates but sometimes the clamor for her was just too loud to be ignored. By now, they were calling, *Manang*, Narita! When it was her turn, she would start in the local language. She could converse passably in tongue twisters like Pangasinan and Zambal and she even picked up a bit of Tausug.

There was nothing intellectual or explosive about her speeches on the road. Soon, the audience would clamor for her to sing and she always gave them "Lahat ng Araw" which she included in her zarzuela. She even had different versions of it; a university poet whom she flattered wrote Ilokano lyrics and she had a journalist from Cebu do it in Cebuano as well. The song became a hit and look at all the record companies doing it in instrumentals and vocals now.

But it was a case of overkill and I don't know whose idea it was—Senator Reyes' or Narita's. Underneath the glossy exterior of that campaign, the music, the fanfare, there was something sinister. And that first meeting with Senator Reyes came to mind.

I am fully aware of course that to go deeper into this is to tread on dark, unfamiliar terra infirma. I can only guess her views on poverty developed because of her childhood; her rejection of the slums afterwards was based not on a sense of moral outrage but on aesthetics. She could not stand the unsightly around her, whether it was a man like me who did not comb his hair or a slum dweller's *barong-barong.*

Her view of the world was, therefore, cosmetic although she, herself, would not admit it.

The violence—and I had reports of it—was committed in many places, in our own town, mostly in our province. A former clerk in the *municipio* had dredged up the fact that her father had absconded with some money. The poor man was beaten up and Father had to treat him for lacerations. She was perhaps determined that in her homeground, she should be on top—which she was not only because Senator Reyes poured a lot of money but because she was the local girl who made good. The opposition mayor of Tubas, close to our town, was killed. It was a shooting "accident" and although people had come to Manila to say it was not, there was no mention of it in the papers. That was the extent to which the papers were manipulated. And vote-buying, bribery, dumping—I will not recite these. It is enough that I knew they happened not because she and her father-in-law were insecure but because they believed in overkill.

With both of them now in the Senate, I thought it was time to push through government progams such as those which we had worked so hard to shape. After the euphoria had died, I got the whole sheaf of proposals together one Saturday morning. It was a full two weeks after the election and I knew that the time was opportune to discuss them for soon the Senate sessions would start.

It was not that I personally was filled with love for the downtrodden, but in that small Negros town, Father had attended to the workers in the farm with free professional care. Mother taught school before she married Father and she tried her best to teach the children who did not attend public school the rudiments at least of writing and reading. Father had always hammered into us that the workers, though they were not as educated as we were, had the same blood. I was not about to organize them into a militant and radical labor union nor was I inclined to shout revolution like some of my colleagues at the university. I think I was too comfortable to do that, but I was not going to see them mired in either perpetual ignorance or poverty. I saw enough evidence in America to show that wealth—when spread around—would do everyone a bit of good.

Narita always called when she needed me, which was often. It was one of those few instances when I called her. "All right, Eddie. Come early enough so we can have lunch," she said brightly.

I had already bought a Volks. Her money was useful and because she was happy with the group, she upped my consultancy fee as she called it to four thousand a month, much, much more than I was making at the university. I had difficulty convincing myself that I really earned it.

She was not yet up when I arrived and it was already past eleven. She had earlier gone horseback riding at the Polo Club then gone back to sleep. By noon, I was served coffee and a plateful of sandwiches and cold yogurt. I was halfway through when she came down in her dressing gown, a shimmery kind, her breasts showing through.

"That is a very sexy dress," I said, thinking about New York again. In the almost three years since, we never had any kind of real intimacy and all the reward I got was an occasional kiss on the mouth, the pressing of bodies, a lingering handclasp. I was in a position where I couldn't expect more.

She took the sandwiches away and told the cook to prepare the table at once. But I already had enough and I barely touched the Chateaubriand. It was a leisurely lunch and I could see that the arduous campaign had not ravaged her; she was as fresh and as lovely as ever. With our coffee, we went to the library. She noticed my bulky portfolio. "It is business then," she smiled.

I recalled our first meeting with the senator in the same room, how we had talked about responsive government and that as she probably saw in her provincial sallies, the first priority was rural poverty, agarian reform, anything to improve the lives of the rural poor. She listened for a few minutes while I mapped out the parameters of legislative action, but soon I could see that she was not concentrating.

"You are not interested," I said with irritation.

"Because I know everything you are saying, Eddie, and right now, I am not really interested."

I never felt as futile and as helpless as I did then, to be told that I was talking to a stone. I gathered the folders and dumped them into my briefcase. Then, more in sadness than in anger: "I had hoped you would remember not just Santa Ana but the things you told me. Am I wrong in hoping you won't be like the rest? There should be conscience in politics, else we would be nothing but pigs . . ."

"Then let us be pigs," she said with a vehemence that startled me. "Conscience, duty—all those virtues that you hear bandied about—my duty is not to God and country. It is to me—myself first, because without myself, what would there be? And look at you, you and your . . . genteel morality—what is it that you look forward to first? Your career, no less. I'm not here to clean the stables, to change tradition—the tradition in corruption. I am part of the herd although very much above the herd. Who can say this with the honesty that I am saying it?"

I could not speak.

She went on. "Listen, Eddie. In these four years, I will do what I can. Only a bit—for my image, for patronage. I am aiming beyond the Senate. Nothing but the top, the Presidency. You understand that? And when I'm there, that's when we can go to town, do all the things you want to do. You think Papa is all that powerful? No, and neither will I be. I would be very pleased if you boys paid some attention to that. Focus on the next election because that's where I'm headed. And I will use everything I can to get there."

"Power has gone to your head," I said. "You're using people as if they were things. Objects. I thought you didn't like America because it is like that."

"I pay them well. I pay you very well. No one can top what I am giving them, or you."

"I'll go back there. To hell with your money."

"You will rot there," she said, trying to be conciliatory.

"That is where I prefer to be. I am a scholar."

"What is scholarship if it is not used?"

"The search for truth is sometimes without use from your point of view. But truth is always useful to humanity at large."

"The hell with humanity. You can love humanity without loving one single individual."

"Are you describing yourself? Remember the Caesars. *Sic transit gloria mundi,* all that sort of thing."

"I am not building an empire."

"There is no difference. You are in love with power. Caesar, when he was paraded in Rome, there was always this man following him, whispering, chanting: 'Remember, thou art mortal.' So Narita, remember—you are full of shit."

"I will have you fired," she said under her breath.

"You will have me flogged. But does that destroy the truth? And the truth is that you're no different from the politicians you despise, from those girls at Assumption who snubbed you. You are snubbing man—and you cannot do that unless you resign from the human race."

"Get out of my sight," she shouted.

"Gladly," I said.

She did not stop me.

Driving on the highway, I was so angry, so frustrated, I

started to cry. I decided then that I would not have anything more to do with her. The four-thousand-peso loss would be a real sacrifice. It had helped with the mortgage on the house. There would also be less money for my sisters who were still in school. To help them was one of my duties as the eldest.

I also got frightened. She could very well carry out her threat to have me kicked out of the university. I had tenure but what was tenure if people with no compassion were in power?

I need not have worried. The following day, bright and early, there she was in her new Mercedes 300. I was having breakfast when I saw the car park in front of the gate. I rushed to my room upstairs and told my sisters to tell her that I was not in.

I could hear her downstairs, her disbelief that I would leave so early on a Sunday morning. She said, "Well, I have nothing to do. I can wait the whole day if it comes to that. And I haven't had breakfast yet."

There was a scramble to prepare for breakfast and I knew how embarrassed and uneasy my sisters were. Then she asked to go to my study. She wanted to look at my books and get something to read while waiting. My attempt at evasion had ended and I padded down the stairs. She grinned, shook a finger, and said, "Eddie—not on a Sunday morning . . ."

She stood up and said she wanted to see my study or my room anyway and before I could object, she was up the flight and holding on to my arm, my sisters looking at us with amusement.

My room was a mess as usual, my rubber shoes in the doorway, my dirty underwear under the desk, my books all over the place, my diploma still unframed and stuck on the wall with pins. As soon as we went in, she turned the latch. Then Narita kissed me deeply, passionately, murmuring, "I am sorry, darling, about yesterday. I hurt you, didn't I? I'm here now to apologize and make up."

And what could I say when drowning in her sweetness?

We fell on my bed. She had taken off her dress and tossed it on the floor. My sisters were probably listening in the other room so I made nonsensical small talk. The bed began to squeak and she said, "Damn!" She pulled me to the floor. It would have been uncomfortable but she rode me expertly and all the anxiety, all the anger were gone. There was only this woman as I had imagined her.

For a while, I fantasized about us living together.

We lay on the floor for a long time, talking, remembering New York, the campaign. We went over the few mistakes that were made and how they would be rectified next time. The challenge to her ambition was formidable when we finally came to it—the Presidency. She said it was within her grasp. She could convince the President not to run for reelection and perhaps jokingly, I am not sure now, she said: "If he will not accede to that, I will just put a few drops of cyanide in his coffee. He drinks it black so he won't recognize the bitter taste."

"How can you talk so complacently and with such familiarity about him?" I asked, turning on my side to face her.

She poked me in the ribs then. "Oh, Eddie, you were really born yesterday! Didn't you know? The President and I—we became lovers during the campaign."

At first, I had thought of limiting my interview with Senator Reyes to his comments about Narita, to his observations on national politics and the contribution his daughter-in-law had made. But I soon realized that this was a mistake for the senator—it's obvious now—shadowed Narita all her life, not like some protective umbrella but as a pall, a fate that started on its course at the time the senator first came to Santa Ana and saw the young *mestiza*.

The interview with Senator Reyes, therefore, is not just central to this story but a document in itself about an era, of the thinking which shaped a generation and the future, and also made the new definition of nationalism and the new public morality. Senator Reyes knew all the prewar political figures from Quezon onwards. He himself had collaborated with the Japanese in World War II and like all the collaborators of that period, justified his acts in the larger interests of the people. He had seen how the same collaborators like him became rich.

To the very end, when he was already approaching senility, he justified himself, what he had done with politics and his brand of self-seeking nationalism. He sometimes castigated the elite to which he belonged for its depradation of the country, for not bringing alternatives to the corrupt political system. But his criticisms were mild and they were not really intended to sink the boat, not even to rock it. He was for the status quo and nationalism would preserve it. But though it is easy to pass judgment on men like him now, Senator Reyes was elevated to his lofty niche in free elections. It was the people who made the likes of him possible and, perhaps, inevitable.

Tape Four

Senator Reyes:

I stand on top of a mountain—I know that you are perhaps thinking, on top of a heap—and you are not wrong, either. You will ask how does one get to the top? Well, it takes a lot of money to do that, and guts. And cleverness, one must never forget that. Those who profess a high degree of virtue, of morality as indicated in the holy writ have no business trying to be leaders or nation builders. They should work in cemeteries, among the dead who cannot complain. I did a lot of complaining, bitching, haranguing in my time. And I am still doing it.

They are all gone now—my children. Yes, I raised quite a good and handsome brood and I had hoped they would grow into princes and princesses, the heirs that I wanted, but this was not meant to be. Still, fate had been very kind to me, to have let me live to this nice old age to see some of my ideological handiwork take root in a country where anything grows. Perhaps it was wrong for me to have laid so much emphasis, or hope, on the family as the shaper of this country's future. Yes, I'm an autocrat, a patriarch, and I saw to it that all those under my wing were protected and those outside—I will not say exterminated—although that is what my enemies thought I was doing. Ignored, that is the word. Ignored! I wanted all of them to go as fast and as far as my vision wanted. They were going to be pillars, not only of the clan. I had seen destiny—we the Reyeses or kings—leading them. I am not His Majesty, although there is really little difference in a country where the family is the beginning and the end.

What is all this talk about revolution, the class struggle? All these I postulated thirty years ago. But how do you really remove the kings? By changing their names and calling them senators? Oligarchs? The intelligentsia agreed with me, they quoted me, they hovered around, partaking of the wisdom which I threw at them like crumbs. I told them nationalism is necessary and the kings themselves must profess it so that they will not lose their heads. It must not be just love of country, but love of people—and here, I mean the lower classes. And that is what I have done, loved the people, worked for them, gave them jobs, direction to their aspirations for dignity, upliftment from the morass in which they had been immersed and which they had come to accept. I raised them up a bit; and in the process, why shouldn't I raise myself higher, too, higher than all of them, the way it had always been? What will happen to the people if they have no leaders?

History will judge me not for what I am, however, and not even for what I have done but for what I have said. This is what goes on the record, this is what is dished out to the masses to read. And there will be scholars in the future as there are today who do not question the documents they read, who do not go beyond the archival presentation of the bureaucracy.

Between the lines, that is where history has always been.

There will always be those, however, who will say that history is written by the strong, but that is not enough: history has to be *believed* if it is to have currency, and believers are what I have always tried to make. There are enough dolts and jackasses among our elite who believe that they are so anointed to rule merely because they have their own propagandists churning out praises for them which, in time, they come to accept as the truth. I was never one of them—I always knew the limitations of power. But at the same time, I was also aware of the cupidity of those men who exercised power . . . Politics has always been accommodation, not uncompromising idealism, although that could help camouflage the real intentions of politicians. This is what I have always told Narita and this, I think, she believed.

What can I say about her? She was my daughter, she was my pupil, she was my heir. All my children—it is not that they have failed me. It was never in their blood—I see that now—to give the nation the service, the thinking that it needed, the way I devoted my life to it. But Narita—from the beginning, I knew that she would do justice to the name she had taken.

If I were only younger . . . but it does not matter. She was some woman, better looking than all the women I have had, and there have been a few . . . She learned very fast, she should have been the first woman president. She got as high as the Senate but even there, look at what she had done, the many programs on nutrition, on culture, on science she had started, the many Centers that were built at her inspiration. Food production has increased, thanks to her, and the sugar workers—although I should not be talking like this—are better off now because of her untiring and unselfish devotion to their cause. Don't laugh—you know that my life had always revolved around sugar, its problems, its world market and, of course, that beautiful quota from the United States. But we were willing to be pushed a bit, not by those mealy mouthed priests, not by those radical labor leaders, but by those whom we trust, who know our feelings, who are part of our constellation. If we give justice to people, we should do so without being prodded and, by God, that is what we did.

These and so many more are Narita's achievements and no gossip monger, no vitriolic critic can take these away.

I knew Narita as a child, I watched her grow; her ideas on nationalism, she got them from me. I was instrumental in shaping them, guiding them. Not that she did not have a mind of her own. In fact she was so independent at times, she could even afford afterwards to antagonize my friends and taunt the whole system itself.

So she has left me two wonderful boys who will not forget their mother as the most heroic, the most unusual Filipina in our history. Gabriela Silang, Tandang Sora, all those revered Filipinas in our lineage—they are really nothing compared to her. The scholars should have no difficulty in confirming this . . .

END OF TAPE

Looking back, I have often wondered about the exact moment when I began to delude myself. I know now that it was done slowly, bit by bit, with my own circumstances and needs, pushing me, my desire to justify myself, that I was really earning the money that she paid me. I also began to believe, towards the latter part of the relationship, that nothing much could be done about our political malaise until she had real power, when she could dictate and no longer have to deal with slimy politicians and make compromises. I realize that this is a fallacy, that government is not a vacuum, that where there are human relationships, compromises are inevitable and that, precisely speaking, the statesman is also a superb politician.

During the first year of her term, I worked hard and there were heated arguments within the think tank for the others were never told—and I never told them—that she was aiming for the Presidency. Of course, that did occur to them. The programs that we shaped always kept her in the public eye. She was a national figure now and well beyond the narrow partisan confines of bloc, of party. She had taken on, too, the nationalist mantle that the aging senator bestowed on her.

It was in the second year of her term that she went to this small college in our province to deliver a commencement address. It was a request she could not deny; besides, it afforded her a chance to see again the old hometown and, perhaps, renew ties. And as the newspapers related it, after she had finished her extemporaneous address on social justice as an ideal she wanted the young to promote, there was a standing and thunderous ovation. It was at this instance, too, that the young graduates all rushed to the stage to congratulate her. It was a mob scene and the stage suddenly swayed and then collapsed.

She had been knocked against a rusty iron truss, there was a gash on her arm—nothing serious, and she was moving around with a sling when she got to the provincial hospital her father-in-law had built.

It was the ultimate irony; a doctor decided to give her an anti-tetanus shot, just to be sure. In seconds, she was gasping in a massive anaphylactoid attack. There was no resuscitator, no antiallergy shot available at that instance. In less than five minutes, she was dead.

These details were ignored by the papers. It was more dramatic to say it was the people's enthusiasm which killed her, that she died in her home ground, defending the rights of the poor sacadas against the rich sugar oligarchs, the applause of the youth her lasting epitaph.

The mythmakers, particularly the PR staff of Senator Reyes, had more than a kernel to start with: The Narita Reyes Foundation immediately came into being purportedly to perpetuate the ideals for which Narita gave her life. Nowhere was it mentioned that the young people had rushed and crowded that flimsy stage for at the end of her speech Narita started handing out those envelopes that were, by then, a familiar gimmick in her public appearances and her campaign . . .

In a couple of years, there floated around variations of her last moments, perhaps to fit the temper of the times. Now, the CIA was responsible. She had been vocal in her anti-Americanism, in her espousal—like her father-in-law—of the removal of the American bases. The CIA saw to it that the stage would collapse!

I knew her well enough to see through her, that like Senator Reyes whose sugar interests survived on American largesse, Narita's anti-Americanism was for the galleries, for the pseudointellectuals of the campuses.

The aides of Senator Reyes woke me up at three o'clock that morning and the senator and I flew to Bacolod in his Cessna, with the casket on board in the back. He was silent during the flight, his crumpled face grown darker with his grief. When we got to the hospital at daybreak, he thundered and raged and said he would have every doctor there forbidden to practice and jailed. We went to the room where Narita lay and at the sight of her, he broke down, the sobs torn out of him in gusts.

They brought the casket in and he forbade them to touch her; only the two of us could. I did not realize till then how light she was. Looking at the quiet face, the eyes closed as if in sleep, the cleft chin, it all came back—the little girl I had played with in Santa Ana, the splashing rain, the ripe guavas and the green cascade of cadena de amor in bloom. I did not want the Old Man to see me cry so I let the tears burn and fall without my wiping them.

She was buried in Manila. Her mother, my parents, and some of our hometown friends who could afford the trip were there. It was a hot April day and we sweated in the hall of the Senate as we listened to the lengthy eulogies.

It was vacation time anyway so after the funeral, I decided to go home with Father and Mother. Our house looked shabby, its wooden sidings in need of paint. I walked over to Narita's new house. It was much more substantial, the biggest house in Santa Ana, bigger than the municipio. The guava and pomelo trees had not been cut but they could not now hide the big house with wooden balustrades and red-painted roof as they had the old house roofed with rusting tin. I don't know if it was on Narita's instructions, but they did not tear down the old brick wall that enclosed the yard and the cadena de amor—now scraggly brown and shorn of leaves—clambered over it. Sometime soon, when the rains shall have started, the vines would be green again.

Sei Thomas Gakuin
Kyoto, April 6, 1979.

OBSESSION

ONE

I hesitate to put down some of the details in this story because they are so intensely personal, they are bound to be misunderstood by friends who know me for my objectivity and detachment, qualities that have made me quite successful in a field crowded by charlatans. Not that my hands are impeccably clean—if we define integrity narrowly, if we polarize the world in black and white, then, certainly, I have not been morally upright. I must avoid euphemisms and say outright that I have been a pimp; for what else is procuring some of the most expensive call girls in town to service clients who have flown in from Wall Street or from Marunouchi? That is precisely what I had done, proceeded to find out who in Didi's stable was available for the evening.

In a way, I am afraid of women. When I was ten, my mother left my father to live with another man. I am now certain that this was the single, most traumatic incident in my life. I worshipped my father and I could not imagine my mother in the arms of another man.

Looking back at what had happened to my marriage I am not surprised that Lydia left me, too, although not for another man, but to flee from the implacable demands of my office, my erratic behavior—as she called it. She had wanted to raise our three children in an atmosphere free from tension and I suppose she succeeded. The kids are grown up now and they seem very normal and happy. Sometimes though, they wonder aloud why Lydia and I never got together again.

My father was not too good at providing for us—he had to work doubly hard at being a surrogate mother and tried to give us a good education, knowing his money would not be wasted. He knew I would be able to make it on my own, from the days of World War II when I was one of the youngest guerrilla officers to fight in the Yamashita campaign. I bore no wounds from that war, other than what scabbed in the mind and heart. I still have the forty-five caliber automatic which I carried then and never used after the war was over. I have not been vicious except, perhaps, once, but this story is not about my war experiences, nor about Media Consultants which I manage, but about my obsession with Ermi.

How could this happen to me at the late age of fifty-five? I have traveled and wallowed in the pleasures of one Babylon or another. I thought I knew all the pitfalls, yet I was shorn of my pride and became naked as the day I was born.

And all because Ermi Rojo was a prostitute.

. . .

Ever since the breakup of my marriage in the early sixties, I have lived in an apartment in Mabini, near Padre Faura. In the early evenings, if I don't jog at the Luneta, I often take a walk along the district's darkened streets. Mabini itself is swept clean for the tourists, as with all of Manila's major avenues, but the narrow sidestreets are awash with the stench of uncollected garbage and human waste oozing out of clogged sewers. Sometimes, I am apprehensive knowing that I may be accosted by hoodlums, beaten up and stabbed. I take a walk just the same almost as a matter of habit, a kind of ceremony with which I welcome the night.

My favorite bar-restaurant, the Camarin—the classiest call girl establishment of them all—has undergone several changes since it was set up in the fifties. It used to serve native cooking, nothing exceptional; then, shortly after martial law was declared in 1972, it became a discreet beer house with first class *pulutan*, including marinated raw fish with generous slices of onions.

The Japanese brought the latest fad to Camarin—the open grill where fresh fish, eggplant and what-have-you are roasted right before the customer. Now, it has a dozen go-go dancers, all young and curvy, who prance about on a narrow stage, in very brief costumes.

I join the night crowd there, the smoke densely floating around, the smell of beer and mankind gone sour comingled with the heat of day. A chubby girl ambles up the stage, her flanks tawny in the yellow light and on her rear the name Gloria. What glory can she possibly bring to these jaded lechers like myself? She gyrates her broad hips, thrusts them towards her audience lasciviously to the rhythm of "Saturday Night Fever," her face without expression. The men talk on, barely giving her a glance.

Didi, my lesbian friend who manages the Camarin, sits at one corner. For more than a decade, she had watched over the place, showing an album of stabled girls only to customers of long standing. She is stouter now than when I first met her. She still regards men as competitors and her eye for feminine beauty is as sharp as ever. It was she who introduced Ermi Rojo to me and that night I met Ermi is permanently etched in my mind.

Two years after I set up Media Consultants, I began to have a bit of time on my hands, time which, I thought, I could use to write. I had set up my Makati office in recognition of that old saying that if you can't lick them, join them. Nationalism is edifying for conversation, editorials, etc., but not profitable in actual practice for as long as the Philippines remains an American colony. This was my experience in the ten years that I worked for B.G. Collas' advertising agency; I saw his outfit dwindle, his accounts taken over by American firms because these accounts were, in the first place, also American.

But I had the right credentials and luck was on my side. Steve Williams, a former classmate at Yale, came to Manila. He was then head of the economic research department of one of the major Wall Street financing houses and he wanted ties with a Filipino firm that would give his company economic intelligence as well as an "in" with Filipino media. There was no such firm in Manila and there and then, he said he would help me start up Media Consultants, in partnership with the New York firm which had worldwide affiliations and whose president happened to also be a Yale man. A rush trip to New York finalized the arrangement and before long, I had several American and Japanese financial institutions as clients. I had always believed that management made more practical sense than book-learned knowledge and in two years, my outfit was efficiently functioning.

I reread my dissertation on the Filipino entrepreneurial elite and realized that it was empty of the insights that I had now. The dissertation never touched on the social vices of this elite, the function of sexuality in determining not just status but, in a far more significant way, how sex influences corporate mobility, the rise and even downfall of businesses through excesses in the ancient *querida* system. This lack led me to delve deeper into Filipino sexuality, from the time of Pigafetta to the present, not just as historical fact but as an expression of our culture.

To put it in another way: Two great thinkers had postulated man's drives and salvation. Marx pontificated on the stomach and Freud on the gonads. I was going to be the "third great thinker"—I would synthesize the two approaches and explain what makes Filipino society, why we behave the way we do.

But postulating was not enough; I needed data, background on the earliest sexual practices of Filipinos, the marriage customs of the ethnic groups and what they could reveal about pre-Hispanic attitudes towards marriage and family. I wanted to find out how our contemporary writers handled sex in their stories, novels, their poetry, how homosexuals influenced culture because of their pivotal positions as movie and stage directors and as couturiers who influenced the wives of the elite. I had some background on the sexual practices of executives, the backrooms of their offices furnished like bedrooms for after-lunch sex. I knew of one powerful brokerage manager who had a covey of women in his shop employed solely to provide him with gratification. One of the girls, as a matter of fact, was there to give him a blow job during the morning coffee break.

The amours of the political elite were flagrant. Some of the men close to our past presidents, from Quezon onwards, shared with me their knowledge of affairs in the Palace. But as my research continued, I realized that I had begun to look at prostitution not as a social condition but as a matter of integrity.

Ermi Rojo taught me this implicitly.

. . .

Since the late fifties, I had been bringing journalists to Camarin. Didi was a handsome woman with a deep throaty voice and heavy unplucked eyebrows. Her lips were rather thin but kissable and I suggested once that I kiss her and she had looked at me with such disgust, I would never forget it.

When I was lonely, particularly after Lydia and I separated, Didi would sometimes suggest a girl. She knew my taste; I wanted them sweet—nothing of the *mestiza* glamor type that other men lusted after. She also knew that I was sometimes repelled outright by commercial sex so she saw to it that the girl never mentioned money which, in the first place, I had already placed at Didi's disposal. And because I liked illusions, the girl and I often went first to any of the restaurants in Ermita, sometimes to Alba's or to the Hilton, then home to Mabini.

One afternoon, I got a call from Didi. "You must come tonight," she said. "You like the intellectual type, a good conversation, that sort of thing. I have a surprise for you."

In fact, there were two surprises. First, the girl she introduced me to was still a virgin. Second, her price was ten thousand pesos.

From my apartment, I always walked two blocks to Camarin. It was one of those hot, airless evenings when it seemed like a stroll through the back of a furnace, I was perspiring freely and though my heart was fine, there was this feeling of being stifled not so much by the muggy heat but, I soon realized, by my expectations.

The Camarin is the whole ground floor of an office building done in the Spanish style, with grilled iron windows and a grilled iron gate flanked by iron lamps. No neon sign atop the door—just a simple brass marker. You pushed the door open and walked into an expanse of red tiles, with tables topped with real cloth, and the head waiter, Pete, in a black suit. Beyond the bar, that is before the stage was built for the go-go dancers, was a piano and a piano player, Ralph Alfonso, who used to be a popular movie producer and band leader but had fallen into difficult times. Now, in his old age, he was banging away at the piano and sometimes playing out of tune. I liked Ralph and I always bought him a drink and left a few pesos on the piano ledge because he always played some of the old songs, "Ramona" for instance.

That night I was at the Camarin too early. It was only eight, and the girls had not yet arrived although there were already some customers dining. Didi was at her usual table near the bar where she could see everything, specially the cash register. If not for her sexual preference, Didi would have now been quietly married to some *hacendero* in Negros where she came from. Her family was in sugar in a big way. She had gone to the Assumption, then to a finishing school in Europe, but she preferred this kind of life. To her, it was not only physically satisfying; she was also able to see, as she put it, humanity in the raw, without pretensions. She told me that many prostitutes were by inclination lesbians, and that they always hated or loathed their men. This was useful information for it helped me to understand Ermi better.

She came in exactly at nine. She wore a bright green dress and as she walked to Didi's table, just about everyone paused to look at her. Her presence was striking, there was elegance in her carriage, yet she was simplicity itself—just a bit of lipstick, her boy's bob shining in the cartwheel lamp above her. She was beautiful in an exotic Oriental way, her eyes alight with laughter, her oval face finely sculpted. A painter like Carlos Francisco would have exalted over her.

I stood up and pulled out a chair for her. "This is Rolando Cruz," Didi said. "I wanted you to have my best customer for your first night here."

"Does he know the price?" She spoke to Didi without turning to me. Though her voice was mellow, there was something final and harsh about the way she asked the question.

"The ten thousand, yes." Didi turned to me with a grin. "Ermi here does not sit at the usual rate of thirty pesos an hour. It is double for her—but keep this a secret or else all the girls will be in an uproar if they found out."

I had my usual table near Ralph so I could tell him what tunes to play. Her shoes were not high heeled; she was just a little over five feet and I was taller but not by much. She wore some perfume, Chanel, I think, and I caught a whiff of it as she turned to tell me that Didi had told her about me. Then, as we sat down: "Why does a man of your intellectual background come to a place like this?"

I did not answer immediately. I had thought it better to ignore her question but after she was seated, she repeated it. Ralph had started to play "Ramona" and the waiter had brought me my usual bourbon with water.

"Coke," Ermi said when the waiter asked her. Then, "You didn't answer my question."

I was pressed to the wall. Honesty would be my salvation. "I have been separated from my wife for some time now," I said, spilling over for some reason. "And I'm to blame. It was not a woman who caused it—it was me, my stupidity, paying too much attention to my job, and ignoring her and the home. It was as if I was not married at all. And now, frankly, I don't want any emotional attachments. Attachments can inflict pain. It's best to be casual about sex. Fornicate without affection, fornication without affection . . ."

She nodded as if she agreed. In the soft light, her skin was pure. In the sunlight, she would look even lovelier.

"What is a pretty girl like you doing here?"

"Money," she said quickly. "Nothing else. And now that we are through with the introductions, you must make the most of your one hour . . ."

"Can I ask you your name at least?"

"Ermi," she said, smiling. "But no family names, no addresses, no telephone numbers. You can always get in touch with me through Didi if you want me . . ."

"You are so businesslike," I said. "Which means that you are new in the business. You turn me off that way. I don't like being hustled. I don't think any man does."

She seemed thoughtful. She brought her chin up, her lips in a pout. "Maybe, you're right. It is my manner, I guess. The directness. Thanks for telling me."

"That's a lot better," I said. "Don't regard me—men—as

your enemy although you will perhaps eventually do that. Some of us can fall in love, too, even with girls like you . . ."

"Oh?"

"Love is blind, or haven't you heard?"

"That's for the birds," she said quickly. "I keep my head all the time."

"Sometime in the future, you'll slip. There are girls right in Camarin who fork over their earnings to boyfriends. They buy cars for their men while they ride in jeepneys."

"That will never happen to me," she said grimly. "All the money I will make will be for me. For me alone."

"And the first is ten thousand."

She laughed softly, that easy laughter which I would always remember. "Actually," she explained, "it will only be five. Fifty percent will go to Didi."

"At that rate," I said, "it will have to be a rich Chinese *sari-sari* store owner who will deflower you. Only they can afford it."

"Do you know one?"

I shook my head.

"And of course, you won't give up ten thousand for one night of the wildest pleasure you have ever known," she said. "Look, I have read several sex books, including that crazy *Kama Sutra*."

"Not on the first night," I said. "You will be in pain."

"But only the first time."

"There will be no second time for me," I said. "I am not a teenager anymore."

"I will make you feel like one again."

"Not for ten thousand. But if you are willing to have it in installments . . ."

She pouted again.

"Maybe, one of my foreign friends. One of these days, I'm certain . . ."

"I speak Spanish, French and, of course, English. A smattering of Visayan and Ilokano, too. Learned them when I was young . . ."

"Good to know about your gift for language," I said.

I told her that the cult of virginity was fast disappearing as sociological surveys at the University of the Philippines and other schools had shown; that it is only the conservative male who still holds to it in the hope that his virgin wife will be more faithful and his ego satisfied.

"Was your wife a virgin when you married her?"

"Of course," I said. Lydia and I had premarital relations but she was a virgin when I first took her.

"And what if she wasn't?" Although the question was hypothetical, it was disturbing just the same.

When I visited Ermi again the following week, she already had a nickname. She was called *Dies Mil*—or ten thousand, and there were still no takers. She was already Camarin's most popular girl and men were often there early so they could have her at their table, watch her, listen to her. I could not get her the second time—a balding, middle-aged man had tabled her the whole evening till closing time but was not prepared to part with ten thousand.

Ermi was brighter than I when it came to analyzing relationships. I had thought that in the end ours would be strengthened by the business that I had brought her. But it was I who brought her the man who paid her ten thousand. She never thanked me for it and looking back I think that she loathed me instead for having started her off.

In the mid-sixties, a "Great Leader" from a neighboring country came incognito to Manila for what seemed to be his last fling. He was suffering from gout, high blood pressure and all the ailments with which frenzied high living ravishes the aging body. I got a call that afternoon from his embassy; he had just arrived and he made it clear to his ambassador that he needed a young girl for the night. The ambassador was a dull, colorless bureaucrat who relied on his cultural attaché for this sort of expertise. I happened to know the attaché—one of the multinationals I represented had interests in his country's massive oil resources and it was natural for me to ingratiate myself with him.

My introducing the Great Leader to Ermi pleased everyone. Two months afterwards, Ermi got a house in Forbes Park and when I saw her again, she was no longer being tabled at Camarin although she still dropped in and made appointments there. Now, she was a prominent item in Didi's stable; she was on call for three thousand pesos a night and in the sixties, that was very good money.

By then, too, I was drawn to the Camarin more often. I deluded myself into thinking that I was really involved with research, amassing new insights from Didi and her girls. It was Ermi, of course, whom I really wanted to see before she stepped out for the night; it was she who, I hoped, would be able to have a little time at my table, crumbs before a starveling.

We were able to talk briefly on occasion and she attended to me, perhaps out of her initial gratitude for introducing her to the "Great Man."

She agreed to go to the Luneta one Sunday afternoon and we met at the Hilton lobby then walked over to the park where there was a symphony concert. It was one of those translucent October afternoons, the sky was clean and blue, and the breeze from the sea was cool. She had on a light maroon dress and white high heeled shoes, and she walked with me rather self-consciously for almost everyone was in casual dress, in jeans, and here she was, strikingly handsome as always, making the plain dress so elegant, people looking at her. "I hope," she said, nudging my arm, "they don't think I am giving a fashion show."

She liked the music, the overtures of several ballets, but we did not stay in the open air theatre long; we moved on to the Chinese garden where we found a stone bench to sit on, watching the people pass, the lovers entwined in each other's arms under the trees in the gathering twilight.

Several people knew of her success by then although she was reticent about it. But we spoke of it anyhow. "Bring me more like him," she said, laughing, "so I can have a dozen houses in Forbes Park."

"And how is your house there?"

She was all seriousness again. "No addresses, no telephone numbers . . ."

"Ermi—still mistrusting men. Even me after all this time. I don't even know your family name and Didi's so loyal, she refuses to give it. Don't I deserve some trust?"

She smiled, her even teeth flashing. "Yes, Roly," she said, pressing my hand. "I think you deserve some trust. My family name is Rojo."

How could anyone miss that? The Rojos were extremely wealthy, an old Ermita family. Their original wealth in land had since the end of World War II been diversified into banking, manufacturing . . .

"I know what you are thinking," she added quickly. "Not that clan of Rojo. I am not even a poor cousin."

"*Was* the poor one," I corrected her. "You are getting rich now."

I was not going to be a judge of her morals. I was no missionary out to vanquish sin from the face of Manila. Still, I said, "When are you going to retire? You can do that now, you know. I hear that the Great Leader gave you blue chip stocks in those companies that have investments in his country."

"Retire? There are still many good years ahead of me. Not while I can command a good price . . ."

I was shocked at the revelation of her vaulting ambition, her greed. I should have loathed her or, knowing what kind of a person she was, I should have realized the futility of any personal attachment, the impossibility of its maturing into something warm, human, enduring. By then, I had known a bit of the prostitute's psychology, the ruthlessness which marked her relationship with men, but I ignored these.

The revelation came slowly and when it finally became clear like sunrise, it seared me—the knowledge that I cared for her, that I wanted her to leave her kind of life. I was not going to tell her how I felt . . .

"Just remember this," I said instead. "In a world grown dark with deceit there are many who are blinded and few who can hold up a light so that we can see the way. More important, so that we can look at ourselves, as well as others, and know how different or similar we are to the herd."

She was bright with figures but the soft talk of the humanities bored her and I was now talking elusively, because I did not want to call her a prostitute to her face.

"You're flattering yourself," she said. "You want to tell me that you are bringing light to dark corners with your kind of truth and that if I see the light, I will change?"

"No," I said. "That is not what I meant. I know well enough that I am cynical. But I am also religious because I am a sinner. Not many can say this of themselves. I accept certain realities which I cannot change. I am not trying to give you a sermon."

"But you are, you know," she said with a turn of the lovely mouth that was almost a sneer. "You're trying to say that I am not a moral person, that you look down on me and, therefore, I should feel guilty . . ."

I did not speak; she knew she was right.

"You and your pompous values," she laughed quietly.

"How can you be so dumb. We are not different, we are very much alike. Go before a mirror, Roly. Ask yourself how you have behaved during the last ten years, or even just during the last ten days. We are alike, I repeat. I sell mine—and you—you sell yourself."

TWO

As Ermi had bitterly suggested, that evening, I went to the mirror—this pallid face, the lines beginning to form around the nose, the wrinkles deepening on the forehead, the graying around the temples more pronounced. I had thought of dyeing my hair but I was just too egoistical to do it, assuring myself that a man is as young as he feels. I asked this man in the mirror, now in the inevitable grasp of middle age, if he was a prostitute, too, and I scanned the bleak terrain of his past, the years with B.G. Collas when he used to sell everything, including soft drinks, with the habiliments of nationalism. So then, Rolando Cruz, Ph.D. in history, do you recall how you composed advertising copy embellished with your knowledge of your country's past? The hortatory speeches you wrote for corporate and government hierarchs who did not really know, much less believe, what you put in their mouths? I justified these as providing my family a home, a good education for the children, a future that would not be wracked by the dismal insecurity and unhappiness that I had known as a boy.

I was now humbled, devastated even by what Ermi had told me. As my conscience, I must see her again. Now, she was behind my mind, insinuating herself, a nagging, unsettling subconscious. I could not concentrate on what was important at hand. I had a staff of about thirty but I had to read all the final reports and correct them if necessary. I initiated research. My foreign clients wanted background on labor conditions, availability of raw materials, political leaders and options for influencing them, loopholes in government procedures and investment laws, taxes—all the information they needed to make profits without sweating.

What had Ermi cast over me? A net? Perhaps a medieval spell, or an *aswang* talisman which would cripple me if I did not run or persevere in cutting myself away from all that reminded me of her. This was, of course, impossible. Everywhere I turned were new restaurants, bars, massage parlors which had started to proliferate and, later on, the new hotels.

Indeed, how Ermita had changed! Marcelo H. del Pilar Street—what would that self-effacing, courageous propagandist say now if he saw that the street named after him had become "sin avenue" festooned with the glitter and shine of pick-up bars. My own Mabini, named after that stubborn and unswerving ideologue of the revolution, has become a raucous arcade of souvenir shops and that genre painting for tourists which portrayed the Philippines as a land of pouring sunlight, elegiac harvestime, wide-eyed children and forever enchanting village girls.

Once upon a time, the whole Ermita area was the precinct of the *mestizo* elite. Plaza Militar and its environs, which I could see from my window, were the compounds of the American aristocracy. These streets were lined with acacias then and behind the high walls of ivy, in the august mansions, was a sybaritic life devoid of the anxieties of colonialism. Then the war came and Ermita was leveled; the *mestizos* and the colonialists left it to form another *ilustrado* enclave in a former grassland called Makati. And their abandoned mansions which were spared, now decrepit and ill preserved, had become tawdry love motels.

How could I ignore Ermi? How could I stop breathing? She was now embedded in my mind, a part of me. I could no longer think. My job demanded a mind free from all these impediments that made it impossible to relate cause and effect.

Cause and effect! There was nothing I did which excluded her. If I went to an appointment in the afternoon or in the evening, would it enable me to pass by Camarin so that I could see her before someone took her out? She had by now a good clientele. There were many offers, she told me, to make her a full-time mistress, to be "garaged" as the expression went, but she was familiar with the liabilities that arose from such arrangements. But what really vexed me was the fact that though she could afford to quit, she still persisted.

I started taking meditation lessons. Indeed, after a half hour of contemplating my feet, my mind would be rid of junk and all thoughts of Ermi that bedeviled me. But only for a while. Soon enough she intruded again. I realized then that I would have to leave Manila—even just for a few weeks—time enough to flee the single subject that had begun to canker me.

The first stop was Honolulu. Lolling on the beach at Ala Moana enabled me to think soberly not only of her but of Manila. It was beginning to wobble under the accretion of ancient problems, a radicalized youth movement battering at the hoary walls of privilege, including the multinationals which I represented and defended. I had sympathized with the demands for change but my bread did not come from kids who massed at the American embassy and rampaged in the streets of Ermita, smashing shop windows and splattering their vaulting slogans on the walls.

I had brought my notes on sexuality and began to work on them, particularly those about the lesbians and transvestites with whom Didi had put me in touch. I was amused, remembering an "international fashion show" by the transvestites at a UN Avenue auditorium the week I left. They were all dolled up and even under those lights, no one would have thought they were men.

Honolulu was, of course, wide open to the changes in sexual mores that had transformed much of American society, perhaps fundamentally. More so was San Francisco which had become the gay capital of America. But my interests were centered on home. America eddied around me, distant, impermeable. I was not involved.

A month in the United States, a month in South America which pitched me up the heights of Machu Picchu, and also one month in Europe—with the exotic food, one-night stands—and I instead—continued to marvel at what had happened in Manila. Had I procrastinated, I would have been enslaved by emotions I could no longer control. Now, I wanted to find something I could latch on to, not just history which had fired me in the past, but something equally immaterial, some ideal that would sustain me in this solitary middle age.

The pleasant deviations in New York, the cherry stone clams at Nathan's, the juiciest steaks at Gallaghers, all the sensual pleasures of Babylon did not, however, waylay memory. I had hoped it would be easy to forget Ermi but the distance only served to heighten my loneliness, my desire to be with her again. What did I recall of our talks? She did tell me she was good at math. Yes, she loved chocolates although sometimes too lazy even just to take the tinsel wrapping off Hershey's Kisses before putting them into her mouth. I began to suspect that, perhaps, I was a masochist, that I was getting satisfaction from the agony that I was undergoing. It was when I slept that I should have had some peace but she obtruded in my dreams.

Then, the three months were over. Back in Manila, I wanted to rush to Camarin but I must test my will. For weeks I did not go although twice in that period, one of my staffers called up Didi for her girls. In the third week, my determination collapsed.

Didi was at her usual table and she asked why I had kept away so long. A business trip, I explained. And Ermi?

"She left about two weeks ago," she said.

I regretted my foolishness. I damned myself.

"For the United States," Didi continued. "You must have missed her a lot."

I nodded. "Will she stay there long?"

"Maybe two months, maybe two years."

It was just as well then, I consoled myself. Her protracted absence, about which I could do nothing, would be my final cure.

Martial law came and for the first time in my operation, everything went awry as the rules were changed. The media targets were more easily defined for there was no longer a free press and all the owners of media were either friends or relatives of the occupant of Malacañang. Gathering economic data was both easy and difficult. All that one had to know was the pattern of new elite relationships, the regions where the entrepreneurs came from. But now, government information sources were very secretive and what were once normal public documents were regarded as state secrets. One clear pattern emerged—the centralization of corruption and a thrust towards the building of infrastructures for export that depressed wages and gave new and dazzling capital sources to a favored few. I had heavily invested in the construction of a modest office building in Makati and put money in blue chip stocks. I was a *segurista*—I was not going to gamble with the little money I had made. Although more multinationals were coming, there was much less work for us now and I was forced to let some of my top people go along with a third of the work force. I also had to sell the office building to meet not just current obligations but the growing inflation. My mistake was not in forging the right connections early enough. In retrospect, even if I had, I would not have been able to do much for I was never really that close to the new oligarchs. They set up a similar company which naturally got all the new businesses plus a lot of what I used to have.

I should not complain too much; I was not badly off in the end, unlike some of my friends in media who lost their franchises, their newspapers and the positions of prestige they once held.

I was soon to see some acquaintances who were virtual paupers in 1966 become multimillionaires in 1976, with newspapers, ranches in Mindoro and timberlands in Palawan, all of them rich enough to buy majority holdings in established companies which the new dispensation wanted to take over.

How easily fortunes have changed, I thought, even for Ermi who had disappeared in the gilded vastness of America. I sometimes called Didi to ask if she had returned, only to learn that she never even sent a card to her madam. Perhaps, by now, she had dropped out of the trade; perhaps I would never see her again. I thought that time and distance would obliterate memories of her; these were the simplest tools with which to drain or cleanse the mind. But these were not enough.

It was a warm March afternoon and I was browsing in my favorite bookshop on Padre Faura when I sensed, when I knew, she was there. She did not see me at the far corner, among the history books, but I saw her at once. Now I realized with a pang both of sorrow and exaltation that I had never stopped caring. I crouched low before the Philippine shelves and moved towards the Asian shelves so I could have a better look. She was going through the samples of wrapping paper for which the bookshop was noted and was admiring a sheet with a big cartoon rendition of an elephant. She was in a green print dress with small yellow flowers, her hair almost brownish in the light. She had slimmed, perhaps by ten pounds. I have never been fond of voluptuous women anyway, leaving those to Rubens or Boticelli. Looking at her, how could I keep away? How could I deny myself again? To be with her was a compulsion, a mesmeric force. The moth flew at the flame.

She was asking the salesgirl how much the sheet cost. I stood up then and went to her, my heart thrashing wildly, my throat as dry as a riverbed in April. I did not speak. She turned, recognized me at once.

"Roly, this is a surprise . . ."

"I am here almost every Saturday afternoon," I said. "I live close by."

"I have not forgotten."

I asked where she was going from the bookshop. She was evasive as usual. I must not lose track of her ever again so I asked if I could take her home but she said no—no one ever took her home.

"I'd like to be your friend, Ermi," I said. I had told her that once before and she had said it was impossible for a man to be a real friend of a woman like her. That friendship would surely end in bed and the relationship would then be irrevocably altered.

She smiled and shook her head.

"Please, I would like to see you again."

"You can always get in touch with me at Camarin."

I was surprised; I had thought she had given up the trade.

"No, I would like to take you out. Tomorrow, Sunday. Anytime you want, anywhere you please . . ."

I went out with her to the street. Her manner was abrupt. "Don't follow me," she said. "I have an appointment. But tomorrow . . ." She seemed to give the idea some thought. "Ten o'clock at the east entrance to Rustan's in Cubao. Do you know the place?"

I nodded. She shook my hand then turned towards Mabini where she hailed a cab.

Ten o'clock. The night before, I barely slept thinking how it would be, the important things I would tell her. She was prompt. She was in blue jeans and a white blouse with red flowers, her face lightly made up. The day was unusually muggy and warm and was, so I learned the day after, the hottest day of the year. Her brow was moist so I let her use my handkerchief.

"Let's go see a movie," she said tentatively. "But I can see one any time. Why don't we go somewhere else instead?"

My whole day was for her. "Let's go to Calamba," I said. She did not know much about Rizal or his novels, and she had not even visited Fort Santiago though she had lived in Manila much of her life.

"Shame on you," I said. "You have no sense of history."

"The past be damned," she said with a viciousness which surprised me.

I asked why she chose Cubao as our meeting place and she said she lived in the area.

"And what about your house in Forbes Park?"

"Don't be silly," she said. "How can I ever live there? I am renting the house out and I have bought a much smaller one."

I knew then that she would not end up selling sweepstakes tickets and said so.

"And what makes you think that I will end up that way?"

"Many of the girls do," I said. "You are good for only a few years. Then you start getting old, wrinkles on the face, the breasts sag. It is then that you get loved for what you are . . . *if* you are loved."

She was silent and that was when I said: "You will find that it will only be one man who will care for you then."

She did not speak, as if she did not hear.

"Ermi," I said, "before you left, I almost went crazy over you. I went away, too, for three months. What did you do in the States?"

"I saw my mother," she said quickly. It was the first thing about her life which she had told me.

"Tell me about her."

Her eyes were imploring. "Roly, please don't ask questions about my family, my past. I don't want to talk about them. It hurts, just remembering . . ."

I did not ask her again.

"I have had many nasty experiences," she said. "I don't want them repeated."

"I promise not to embarrass you."

"I know that. But in the future, I am sure to meet these men again and there will be phony explanations to make."

"I am not ashamed to be seen with you," I said and meant it.

She pinched my arm. We were now on the highway to Calamba, bright and wide and hot. "I am sorry," I said. "This ten-year-old Mercedes is not air-conditioned. I am not rich and martial law has been very unkind to me."

"You need not apologize," she said. "Just don't take me to those ritzy places where there are many people. I am ill at ease there. I would rather go out at night, with no one seeing me, knowing me. I am tired having to look down, always avoiding the eyes of people."

It all came back, the darkness being kind, hiding as it does almost everyone. I never knew and perhaps will never know what got her started in Camarin. But I do know that if money was the reason for her having started, it was not valid now as the cause for her return. "I am disturbed but glad because I can see you again. Why did you go back, Ermi? I thought that with your success with the Great Leader, the house in Forbes Park . . ."

"Are you going to give me a sermon again?"

"You are too old for that and I am too tired to give one. Besides, who am I to make judgments?"

"But you don't approve of my going back, I know. Well, no one forced me in the beginning. And no one forced me to return, if that is what you want to know. I did it by myself."

I told her that relationships in Camarin had a certain attraction, a magnetic pull to those who were there. Friendships, very strong bonds at that, were created. Her return was certainly welcomed by the girls there for it confirmed, it justified them.

"You are right," she said. "But it was still my decision and I am answerable to no one but myself."

The old highway was clogged with traffic and in the midday heat, she looked fatigued. I was relieved when we reached Calamba and parked in the acacia-shaded yard of the church where we went before visiting the old Rizal house. I told her about the *ilustrados* and Rizal's Sisa and her two sons. The old house, how it was designed and maintained, fascinated her. She marveled at the number of fruit trees in the yard. She was interested in house-plants and on the way back, we stopped on the highway and I bought her a potted palmetto which I placed in the back of the car.

It was almost four in the afternoon and still hot. "I can drop you off in Cubao where you can get a taxi," I said. "I know you don't want me to bring you to your gate."

She was quiet again for a time. We were now in Cubao and I turned to the right, to the Farmers Market parking area.

"You can take me home," she said. "But promise not to get out of the car when we get there."

Her house was in a small side street. It had high walls and a black, iron gate with a lock. She had a key and in a while, a boy came out and took the plant. I caught a glimpse of her bungalow and its yard green with plants.

"When will I see you again?"

"Next Sunday, late in the afternoon, if you are free," she said. "I want to see Fort Santiago."

I returned to Mabini convinced that I could not now free myself of her. Now, I wanted a definition of love not circumscribed by the sexual act for it had become mundane, a commerce bereft of those nuances for which a man would commit murder or suicide. Copulation was no longer an expression of love. While it was not sordid, it had become a measure of one's wealth. The more I needed it, the more I had to pay. With Ermi, how then should I express myself? There are, of course, more profound ways of saying it, the immersion of the self in compassion. Love which is true after all demands no rewards, no favors. How easily I understood now that it is better to give than to receive.

But what could I give her? It was money she wanted most, which led her to Camarin and that commodity was not now easily available to me.

I took her to the old fort that Sunday evening shortly after nightfall. The walls were bathed with light and in the expanse before the entrance were people enjoying the cool night air. Some excavation was being done where the old moat was and they had dug up World War II relics, helmets of Japanese soldiers, bones. The Rizal cell was closed so we meandered to the top of the fort where I showed her the section of the Pasig where the galleons used to set sail for Acapulco. I pointed out the old Parian across the river and close by, the landmarks of Spanish sovereignty, the Manila Cathedral, the Archbishop's Palace, the *Ayuntamiento*—where these used to stand. Then we went down the broad stone steps to where this solitary cross stands, a marker for the hundreds of Filipinos who were killed by the Japanese in the fort. She read the inscription intently and for a time, seemed engrossed in her own thoughts, then she asked, "Were the Japanese really all that bad during the war?"

Her question startled me. I had thought all along that Japanese brutality in World War II was taken for granted. But she was not old enough to have known the Occupation so I told her how it was, my own experiences, the campaign against Yamashita. Quickly, it came hurtling back, those iron cold, rainy nights in the mountains beyond Kiangan, the ribbons of mist that clung to the floor of the valleys in the mornings, and the Japanese—cornered, starved, demoralized—but still fighting viciously where we found them.

It was now thirty years after Yamashita had surrendered but the Japanese never really lost that war. They are back in full force, with their transistors, their lusts. And what had happened to the brave men who had stood up to them once upon a time? The survivors have all become obsequious clerks, and I was among them.

I almost did not get out of that valley; one night, they came down the mountain, slithering on the grass and tossing grenades all over the place. "I was lucky, " I said aloud. "Thanks to an old forty-five which I still keep . . ."

I've had this unlicensed gun for years and almost shot an American advertising client with it. When martial law was declared and the government demanded the surrender of all guns of high caliber, I hid it instead in a more secure place—under the panel, close to the floor, of my bookshelf.

"Now, you know it," I told her. "I hope you will not report me to the Constabulary."

"I can blackmail you," she said brightly. Then her face clouded and she seemed pensive. "Each one of your generation seems to have a Japanese horror story," she said. "Will you believe it, will you be horrified if I told you that my father was a Japanese soldier?"

I gazed at the bright brown eyes, the serene face, and briefly, there came to mind, the faces of the Japanese dead which we had left at the Pass, their bodies bloated, their uniforms rotted. I remembered, too, the neatly uniformed officers—in gold braid, swords by their sides, brown leather boots shiny in the sun—and here she was, claiming kinship with them. If this was 1945, I don't know how I would have reacted—perhaps with more than loathing. But this was 1974—and for many of us, the war was no more than a memory. What was done was done.

Still, I was more than surprised. "Looking at you, and being with you like this—it is difficult to believe," I said.

I knew so little of her past and every bit about it that she revealed had an aura of fiction. Could this be one of them? I did not know where she was born, or anything about her education, but because she spoke French and Spanish, I was sure she was not educated in some diploma mill or cheap public school. If her father was a Japanese soldier, how come then that her family was Rojo, not Yamamoto or some such? However, I had no choice but to believe her for I was certain she was not lying or making up a story.

On our way out, we passed couples necking in the dark, behind abutments in the old wall, on the grass, almost everywhere and she said it was the first time she had seen such sights.

"They have no money," I said. "Perhaps, they are students or office workers. If they had money, they would go to the motels."

"Would you like to take me to one?" she asked, holding on to my arm.

"Of course," I said. "But I cannot afford you. Only my clients can and they can write it off their income tax as entertainment. I am heavily in debt."

"Coward," she whispered as she pulled me to an empty bench near the fountain. And it was then that she asked, "Roly, do I look like a prostitute?"

It was a question I least expected from her, this girl who was brash, who was rich now and who made playthings of men. She had always dressed with simplicity, she was bright, she talked intelligently. It was an instant wherein her life, the sorrow she had to bear, suddenly became luminous and clear. I wanted to embrace her, protect her; it was a feeling completely shorn of desire. It was truly, sincerely love.

"No, Ermi," I said. "You don't look like a whore. You will make a man very happy one day . . ."

"I want to get out," she said. "Start a new life. I know how to cook a bit, and bake. One day, you should taste my chocolate cake. It is my favorite. I will open a small restaurant, I don't know where. I will make a different kind of living."

Her dream gladdened me. She had a future mapped out and it would not be in Ermita. She had started there, she would not end there. I had talked with bar girls, sauna parlor attendants along M.H. del Pilar Street and all of them went into prostitution with the same squalid story, of having been left by their husbands or boyfriends to care for their babies, of having to support brothers and sisters or parents who were no longer capable of earning a living. There was no one I met who went into the trade out of a strong psychological need or for the love of sensuality itself.

I returned to Padre Faura and bought a dozen cookbooks, the best recipes as concocted by the outstanding chefs of Europe. I also got books on how to make canapés, desserts, salads. Now, all she needed for her restaurant was the staff.

I was sure that she already had the money to start a modest one. I drove over to Cubao with the bundle and knocked on the iron gate. Her maid recognized me and opened it. I did not linger as if waiting for an invitation to come in.

That night, while I was working on my notes on sexuality in our folk songs, the phone rang.

"Thank you for the books," Ermi said gaily. "When I start that restaurant, you will be my official taster."

"Thanks for the job," I said. "I wish you would assign me something less meaningful. After all, I cannot be your sugar daddy . . ."

Before Christmas that year, there was another influx of inquiries from American financing institutions and one of my visitors included Andrew Meadows from Atlanta, a clean-cut type with teeth good enough for a toothpaste ad, and reddish hair. He was in his late forties. One evening, while we were having dinner at Bon Vivant in Ermita, he was musing aloud about how he was put off by one of the girls he had brought to his room at the Hilton. That same evening, I sent him to Camarin. It was obvious that he was extremely pleased after the Camarin introductions for he never bothered me again about his asinine evenings.

We did talk, however, about how different Filipino hookers were compared to those in the United States. "There is always something very feminine about them," he said. "Most of those in America are just plain hustlers. They never give men a chance at either illusion or romance . . ."

He was also amused by the government campaign against "indecent" publications, pornographic movies which were really tame compared to what was shown in New York. And it struck him as outrageously foolish—having to blot out the shapes of guns, knives and other weapons in movie ads when these were recognizable anyway. I told him such campaigns were often a camouflage for the insincerity and insecurity of our highest officials. We have always been earthy like all people in feudal, agrarian societies. We who are close to the land regard sex and procreation as natural as eating. Take any village boy; he will recite limericks that are obscene by middle-class standards. All the folk songs I learned when I was young were obscene but no one objected to them, least of all government officials.

In prewar Manila, the highest officials lived graciously, visiting houses of pleasure that offered them relaxation otherwise not available in their own bedrooms.

There is something revolting about photographs of people doing what they should in the privacy of their bedrooms. What is objectionable is not a matter of morality but of taste and, in this sense, the public display of private parts and functions. Magazines like *Playboy* are sold openly in Manila's plush hotels, in Angeles. Porno shops in Tokyo, London, in Scandinavia and, of course, New York's Forty-second Street operate for adults. They are seen not as evil but as aesthetic nuisances which, in truth, they are.

The obscenities in this country are not girls like Ermi, either. It is the poverty which is obscene, and the criminal irresponsibility of the leaders who made this poverty a deadening reality. The obscenities in this country are the palaces of the rich, the new hotels made at the expense of the people, the hospitals where the poor die when they get sick because they don't have the money either for medicines or services. It is only in this light that the real definition of obscenity should be made. There is so much dishonesty today, not just in government but in business. Perhaps, sex is the only honest thing left.

I believed in these conclusions but, looking back, I realized that I had not really done anything to buttress my thinking with action. I served the Establishment, the multinationals—promoted their welfare, and they held no responsibilities at all towards the banishment of our poverty. They were here to make money and nothing else. It was to their advantage that we remained poor, but since I was working for them, I had become comfortable.

In any case, I finally had three thousand pesos. I missed a few luncheon dates, scrimped on supplies, cut corners. I had a meeting in Baguio and I asked Ermi to go with me. "It will cost you a little bit," she said, half mockingly.

I seldom drove to Baguio by then not only because the price of gasoline had soared but because I no longer trusted the old Mercedes to go that far without breaking down. She had told me that she would be at the bus station at seven-thirty and it was the longest thirty minutes of my life, waiting in that narrow room. She did not arrive and ruefully I went up the bus alone. When I arrived at the Pines that afternoon, the first thing I did was to place a call to her house—something I never did before because she told me never to call the number which I had inveigled from Didi.

"I overslept, Roly," she said apologetically.

"Can you catch the three o'clock bus this afternoon?" I asked. "I will be at the station to meet you."

"I will be there."

It was only seven but I was already at the station, braced by the coolness of the mountains. What had attracted me to Ermi? I had asked this of myself every so often. Perhaps, it was her eyes—vibrant and clear and yet holding so much melancholy. I prided myself in the magnitude of my experience. I had told her that it was just as well that I was emotionally and intellectually mature so I could accept the reality of what she was. But if I had been twenty or so, without the understanding which only age and experience can create, I would probably have gone mad just thinking about the men she had. Or, being unable to accept this, I would probably commit suicide.

It began to drizzle; waiting for her in the rain-washed station, these thoughts rankled again. Then it was eight and still no bus. I began to wonder, a clamminess in my hands even as I crossed my fingers. Had the bus fallen off one of those ravines? Had she taken it at all? Other buses arrived, their headlights bright on the pavement, disgorging their passengers into the night. One finally drew in. I saw her as she came down, trim in her blue jeans and white silk blouse, her plastic high-heeled shoes gleaming momentarily in the glare of headlights. She held on to me with the cozy familiarity of a wife and we walked to the Pines close by. She just had-an overnight bag which contained an extra pair of jeans, a couple of T-shirts and over her shoulder, a brown leatherette jacket.

I was going to take her first to the coffee shop so she could have something warm in her stomach but she said she was full, she had eaten a sandwich in Tarlac and wanted to go to bed immediately because she was tired.

The room had twin beds. I was not too sure that she would want to share a wider bed because I snored, but she would have none of that so l pushed the two beds together. Then she said: "Don't leave me alone. I am afraid."

I thought she was just making a professional gesture, a commercial caress, but she added quickly that she could get into a panic in this strange room if left alone. Even as she spoke, she started to breathe heavily. I wondered if she was doing this to turn me into manageable putty in her hands, if there was some reason in her clever mind that I did not know or could not know. I was quite alarmed when she said that if she fainted or went into hysteria, I should give her a glass of water immediately. I held her close, felt her body tremble.

It was sometime before she really calmed down. But by then, she had become sullen. She went to the bathroom and then came out in her pajamas, her breasts showing through the transparent blouse. She sat on the edge of the bed, and did not move. I went to her and explained that I just did not know how to react to her. She just sat there, motionless, a block of wood. Then she turned, a smile breaking on her face, and kissed me.

It was our first and I let it pass like a whiff of wind upon a desert.

"Roly, please don't think I am trying to be difficult," she said after a while. "But I am like this—when I am angry, or very sad, or very frightened. I remember, when I was a child, I'd just keep silent when I was angry—and then, everything would turn black. Even now, at home, my family pampers me and everyone tries to protect me. Still, it sometimes happens—and then when I become conscious again, I realize that someone has bitten my thumb to revive me. My thumb would hurt after that. But what can I do? Will you remember that?"

"The world is too much with you," I said. "I will keep problems away from you . . . if I can. But remember this: We cannot run away. We have to face them sometime. To live with ourselves . . ."

She lay beside me, her breathing now quiet and slow, and as she kissed me again on the cheek, somehow, I could not quite forget that I was just another hunk of flesh, no different from all the others who had loved her. I was determined to hold back, not because I did not want to spend the three thousand pesos—she had consented to come and that in itself was a binding contract. But by not possessing her, this was the only way I would be different; I was going to transcend the act which had, to her, become a commonplace thing. It was difficult, of course. I desired her, this union, this fullest expression of affection. But what would it do for me?

I recalled a massage parlor attendant I had interviewed much earlier; she was building a house somewhere in Pasay and the house was not yet finished. Looking at the windows that lacked shutters, at the kitchen that still had to be tiled, she had told me that she wondered aloud how many more men she would serve before her house would be finished. I was not going to be either a tile or a shutter in her restaurant. I wanted Ermi to remember me as a man who loved her not with his money, of which I had little, but with his heart.

Perhaps it was masochism as well. I asked her to tell me about the lovers she remembered best and she started talking breezily about them. There was one customer she pitied afterwards for he had spent a sizable sum on her. His wife had hired a detective to trail him and succeeded in producing some photographs of Ermi getting into his car. The wife knew where they usually met and she went there ahead of her husband and talked with her, begged her rather to set him free. "Which I did," Ermi said proudly, "but only because his wife was so nice and decent about it all . . ."

By midnight, we had not yet made love. Her head nestled in the crook of my arm and the warmth of her nearness drugged me into blissful silence. Then she said it, without warning, without the pretense that must have always accompanied her behavior with men. "I am so unhappy, Roly. Sometimes, I just sit by myself, wondering how I got into this . . ."

I gazed at the lustrous eyes, the finely molded face, the lips slightly parted. I never knew her as she was now, the belligerence drained from her, the mask finally torn away. At last she was herself, insecure and, I think, wracked by feelings of guilt. She was being honest with me the way I was always honest with her. I had told her of my unhappy childhood, which I never told anyone, the detestable things I had to do to make a comfortable living. I had also told her that if she could not love me, she could, at least, trust me. Did she trust me now? And why should she when I was a man of words? When I had used words as a veneer—shiny and brimming with guile—while underneath them was the dark intent?

I wanted to comfort her, to let her know that if all others would condemn her, I would not.

I had never expected a moment like this when it would come easily to me, the capacity to give shape to this seeking. I uttered the words hoarsely, surprised that I said them at all, that I meant them, that this woman whose body belonged to everyone who could afford it would now be the object of my faith.

"Ermi, I love you."

I was sincere and knowing this sent a cold chill to my marrow. What has happened to me? Had I, in this one moment, forgotten what she was?

She did not stir; she seemed lost in some limbo.

"Ermi, I love you."

She sighed. She had heard the words all too often and they must have lost their meaning. Turning, she kissed me on the chin. The gloom in her face vanished and in its place, this glow of contentment. Somehow, I had succeeded.

"*Bola,*" she said, smiling.

"With your experience, you know it is not *bull.*"

She did not speak for some time. "I have never loved anyone," she said finally.

"I don't expect anything from you, " I said. It would be that way. "I am not young anymore. I am not rich, I cannot give you anything. I am not handsome . . ."

"I was never impressed by handsome men," she said

pinching my shoulder. It had become a habit with her and though it hurt a bit, I let her.

"All that I am, all that I can give—it's like rain fallen on stone."

She did not understand, she asked me to explain.

"Rain which falls on the ground, on the parched earth, brings life. The seeds grow into plants, into harvests. But not rain which falls on stone. Nothing grows on it."

She kissed me again, a wet kiss and I wondered about all the men to whom she had given that token of affection.

"You are my precious piece of rock," I said. "But have you heard of the Chinese water torture?"

She was now an avid listener. "No, tell me."

"Well, water has power, too. The Grand Canyon—you must have also seen those seashores with the stone cut and polished by the constant battering of waves. Erosion. Right on Kennon Road— those big rocks cut by water . . ."

"The Chinese water torture, does it operate on the same principle?"

"They strap a man to a seat and directly above him there is this pail of water with a tiny hole. Water drips slowly, drop by drop, on the man's head, on the same spot . . ."

"It would take ages for that kind of water to break his skull," she said.

"It is not that way," I explained. "The drops come slowly, they make a sound inside the man's brain. He waits for them. Waiting is agony, and when the next drop comes, it is an explosion which gets louder, louder, louder. He is driven insane . . ."

"Is that what you will do to me?"

"This does not work on stone," I said.

She was surprised, of course, when I really refused to touch her. For a moment, perhaps she suspected that I was impotent had she not felt a stirring in my loins when her hand had wandered there. I assured her I would not cheat her of her money and she laughed at this. Then turning on her side, she was soon breathing deeply, and then she snored, too, lightly.

THREE

The mountain cold seeped through the shuttered windows and she snuggled closer. Through stretches of wakefulness, I watched her face in repose; looking at her quiet in sleep, I felt all desire ebb away and in its place this ineffable tenderness. I wanted to enfold her, to shield her from the ignominy that we both knew. I had never experienced this feeling before; it warmed me, filled me with wonder, a strength to do anything to give her joy, to protect her—yes, except how could I protect her from herself?

Once during the night, she roused me with her mumbling. She was moaning softly. I woke her up. "Ermi, is something the matter?"

Her eyes opened and they were frightened. Her arms shot up as if to defend herself and she said aloud, "Don't—don't!" then she realized that it was me.

"I was having a bad dream, " she said, her arms now tight around me. "I feel so weak . . ." For some time, she just lay beside me breathing softly, her eyelids fluttering. I held her hand and found her pulse beating very fast. "I am all right," she assured me. "I was being pushed off a cliff—and I was fighting back."

It was almost daybreak, mayas were chirping on the sill outside, and she slept a little more. The best time to look at a woman, to find the truth about her inner beauty, is in the morning when she wakes up. Ermi's face, even with the wash of sleep, was appealing in its simplicity.

We breakfasted in our room—fried rice, eggs, ham, coffee and a slice of papaya. Then we went out to buy her a pair of walking shoes. Her high heels were not made for the inclines of Baguio. She bought a bunch of bananas—their skins clear yellow and untarnished. "They are so pretty," she said. "I will just look at them first. " I also bought her a rattan shoulder bag. After the market we did Mines View Park, Burnham, the souvenir shops. I took pictures of her all the way but she insisted that I give her the film when the roll was finished, which I did.

There was a carnival on the grounds of the Pines and we lingered there on our last night. It was brightly lit, throbbing with music, but there were so few people, it was pathetic. It was, after all, the last days of the dry season and Baguio would soon be bereft of vacationing crowds. She tried her hand at the darts and then at a shooting gallery and was rewarded with two small packets of mentholated candy. Above us, the Ferris wheel was still but there were people at the roller coaster which had started and was soon clattering noisily above us. "I am scared of that," she said. "In Manila, when I first took a ride in it, I screamed and ordered it stopped . . ."

We talked again till past midnight. I was now sure that it was I who was in a roller coaster, that there was no stopping the ride, and that in the end, it would not ease down but zoom up instead into that gray, terrifying space from where there can be no returning.

She was in my arms again, her hair upon my face. She always turned away after a prolonged kiss and I suspected it was my breath she did not like. This time, I held her face and probed her mouth. She did not open it.

"For whom are you reserving it?" I asked.

"You are too much," she said, sticking out her tongue at last. The taste was of honey salt. "There, " she said. I looked at her eyes that had dredged from me my deepest secrets, my regard for myself and I realized that with her, I was shorn of armor and shield. I did not know till then how vulnerable I had become and I was afraid lest she take advantage of me.

We had begun, surely there must be an ending as well. "Ermi," I said softly, "please don't make a plaything out of me. Should there come a time very soon when you don't want to see me anymore, just say so. I will stay away."

"What are you saying?" she asked.

"With you, I have no pride," I said. "It seems as if I had given you a knife and said, kill me. If that time comes, please make it swift."

"This is all very melodramatic," she said. "But it never entered my mind."

I bent over and kissed the line of her neck, her breasts.

"Thank you," I murmured.

"What for?"

"For being kind."

"That is not difficult to do," she said. "Now, shall we make love?"

I looked lingeringly at her. I shook my head.

She raised herself on her elbows, hugged me and whispered, "Thank you."

After breakfast in our room, I got her bag from the dresser and placed the envelope in it. "What is that?" she asked.

"My contribution to your restaurant."

She took the envelope and gave it back. "But we didn't do it," she said. "You don't owe me anything."

"But I do," I insisted. "You gave me two nights."

"I had free lodging. I did some sight-seeing and had one of the most engaging conversations in my life. No, you don't have to give me anything."

"If I did not do it, it was not your fault."

She grinned and pinched me. "All right then," she said,

"if you want your guilt feelings eased. " She tore the envelope open, picked out a few hundred pesos bills without counting them, and placed them in her bag.

My first meeting was to be in the evening. There was time for me to go to Manila with her then return to Baguio.

"You don't have to. It is such a tedious trip."

"I want this suffering," I said, shushing her.

We sat together in the bus and on occasion, her hand would rest on my thigh or she would hold my hand as we talked. As in the night when she arrived, the first rains of May were upon the land. They came in sheets over the plains of Pangasinan that had started to green. "See what rain does to a land that is parched," I said.

She pressed my hand.

"You make plants grow," I said. "When your gate opened, I caught a glimpse of your lawn—the plants looked very healthy."

"I love gardening," she said.

I remembered the people in her house. "Who are those living with you? Relatives?"

She shook her head. "A driver and his family . . ."

"But you have no car."

She smiled again. "No, he stopped driving a long time ago. He is old now. His wife and children—and grandchildren . . ."

"And you are not related?"

"Not blood relations, but something more real. And there is a girl. She was like me, you know. But she became a drug addict. She has a daughter and she cannot work anymore. She has lost her looks, you know what I mean."

"And you work for them?"

She did not speak. "They are my family," she said simply.

"You are a good girl, Ermi."

"Flattery will get you somewhere," she said.

After our first weekend in Baguio, I noticed a change in my attitude towards the girls in Camarin. Although I still needed them to service my clients, I dropped Ermi from my list. I still went there and sat with one of the girls for drinks or some banter and though the urge was often strong, I started sublimating it with meditation, with my writing. I no longer brought any of the Camarin girls to my apartment. It was easy for me to understand why; though I never told her, it was my regard for Ermi that inhibited me. I just did not feel right anymore making it with any of them, and not because I had abstained from Ermi, either. Maybe, it was a form of loyalty, and considering Ermi's work, it could easily be misconstrued as a perversity. I had never believed in man's monogamous nature and had rather presumed that my sexual needs could never be leashed. Now, I understood how it could be done, without compulsion, not by religious sanctions, not by social constrictions but by that self-willed and strongest bond of all. The knowledge of what love could do gladdened me, surprised me. I was not too old to learn.

The Puesto opened the following year in November. Ermi leased a corner lot on Pasay Avenue, close to Makati. The restaurant was small compared to the plush establishments in the area. Fortunately, the adjoining lot was empty and she promptly rented it for parking. I helped her with suggestions, the decor, how to make good coffee so that people would go there for it and cakes as well. It did not specialize in any particular cuisine. What was offered was almost like home cooking and it could be French, Italian, Chinese, Spanish—whatever was available fresh from the Quezon City markets where she did the shopping herself.

There was nothing pretentious about the Puesto—the tiled front roof, the grilled door, the picture windows which were curtained in the lower portion so that one could have a view of the inside but not of the people eating. The chairs were comfortable, the napkins were of white cloth, the tablecloths in dark red. Ermi's houseplants were all over the place—trailing lantanas, parlor ivy, orchids—hanging from the ceiling, in corners, lush and jungly in the doorway. They gave the Puesto its ambience. She hired a pretty hostess from the University of the Philippines while she herself sat in the booth near the cashier where she could not readily be seen by the customers but where she had a view of the kitchen around the corner, the small bar, and the counter for cakes and pastries. The baking was done right on the premises and the cooking which she often supervised was in a spotless kitchen that was half exposed to the customers so that they could see the food being prepared through glass panels. Even the comfort room was spotless. She had a passion for cleanliness as she, herself, took good care of her personal hygiene.

The inauguration of the restaurant was very quiet—just me and her "family" whom I met for the first time.

But even after having gone out with her several times, what did I really know about her? That she was born after the war but would not tell me her birthday. That her mother was in America, that her father was a Japanese soldier although there was hardly any trace of Japanese in her features except for her clean, creamy complexion which she could have gotten from her mother. She had a house in Forbes Park which she rented out. She was easily scared and could get hysterical. She had, she said, "executed" all the men who loved her after she had gotten what she wanted or after the affair had become sticky. I had nothing—just memories. She had not given me a copy of the pictures I took of her in Baguio although she showed them to me. It is not that I regretted giving her small things, a box of chocolates, a book of crossword puzzles, or records when I returned from Hong Kong.

I suspected that through the few times that we had been together, she had begun to confide in me. I had tried to learn more about her from Didi but Didi was an impregnable repository of secrets. She was now preparing to immigrate to the United States; she had tired of what she was doing in Camarin but more than that, she was beginning to reel with the onslaught of the malaise that had battered most of us, the dishonesty, the deceit that pervaded public life and business as well. "I gave you her phone number, Roly, something I have never done—and only because I know you love her. What you need to know you must get from her. Is her past really all that important since you love her?"

It was not; I took Ermi as she was.

We went to Baguio again. Now, I felt guilty, using up her time without her profitting from me. I owed her a lot now. I was no different from the traditional tenant farmer, forever indebted to his landlord, a serf who can no longer pay his debts in full no matter how hard he works.

Again, I held back. She was amazed at my self-control; she said no one would believe that we had shared a room just so we could talk. But that was what really happened.

By then, her restaurant was flourishing. I hoped that she had already stopped her kind of living but there were evenings when I dropped by the Puesto and she was not there. When I called up her house, she was not there either. I would then be torn with anxiety, anger even, wondering who had taken her out and to what hotel. She had told me to blot these from my mind and I had tried. God, I really tried but it was not possible.

We were at Mario's that early evening, this restaurant along Session Road, and she had ordered spaghetti with meat sauce which she liked very much. She was feeling naughty. "Always remember," she said half seriously, within earshot of the waiter who was showing me the dressings for the chef's salad, "that I am collecting men, just as you are collecting memories."

"Even now, you are playing with me," I said.

She looked at me, the mischief gone from her eyes. "No, Roly, " she said. "I am not playing with you."

"How long has it been?" I asked myself rather than her. "There is no waking hour that you are not in my mind—during the day, even when I am engrossed in my work, and at night when I am in bed. All of a sudden, you are there and when I close my eyes, I can see you." There was another thought which riled but I did not want to plead or beg. "So, when my time comes, let me prepare the coffin at least . . ."

She looked down and was silent. Close to the window, by the street, a Filipino boy and two American girls were having fun and their laughter seemed to fill the whole restaurant. When Ermi raised her head again, she looked at me and in the flicker of that single candlelight, her face was all seriousness. "I think of you a lot," she mumbled and then, as if disturbed by her confession, she started working the spaghetti into her fork and shook her head slowly as if she wanted to deny what she had just uttered.

It was more than I had asked or hoped for. It seemed as if in that tenuous instant, all the burdens that had weighed me down were finally lifted. In the many times that we had talked, she had always been this solid rock, an enigma, and there was so little of her thoughts that I could divine, the real feelings that moved her. Was she finally thawing to become the woman I coveted and not the Ermi who was sought after by everyone at Camarin? I was in a state of euphoria, eating my salad without really tasting it, when a man walked to our table.

"Ermi," he greeted her, holding her shoulder, all attention on her as if I did not exist. "Fancy seeing you here."

She turned to me. "This is Andy Meadows, Roly."

Andy glanced at me and grinned. "We have met," he said, winking. I stood up and shook his hand. He was at ease in the heavy army jacket he was wearing. More niceties, he would like to join us but a couple of his business associates were coming. When he finally left to take a table close to the window, Ermi said simply, "He has proposed to me . . ."

It was difficult for me to believe it, but then, Americans are romantic and are capable of such things. "What do you know of him?" I asked.

She smiled but did not reply.

"Do you think he is serious?"

"I can take care of myself," she said brightly. "No one—and absolutely no one—can make a plaything of me." She had perhaps noted the belligerence in my voice. "Besides, you are jealous."

"The hell I am," I said. "And it was I—of all people, who sent him to Camarin. Will you accept him?"

Her hand slipped up my thigh and she pinched me. "It is a very tempting offer and it is difficult to resist. But I don't know."

That same week, I called Steve Williams in New York and asked him to run a check on Andrew Meadows. It would cost a bit but to me it was important. By the end of January, the report arrived by airmail—a manila envelope thick with information. Ermi received the news with alacrity; in an hour, she was in my apartment. I handed her the folder which I had already gone through and she dug into it avidly. She started with the curriculum vitae, then the other bits of information, copies of press clippings, some duplicate photographs including that of his wife who had just divorced him. Sometimes, as she read, a smile would wreath her face and she would exclaim, "Why—the son of a bitch, he did not tell me this . . ." Or, "Ha! So that is the way it is . . ."

Andrew Meadows was genuine and I was happy for Ermi that she had finally found a man who wanted to marry her. Still, I had to be sure so I asked her, "Does he really know—I mean, your past?"

She laughed, a throaty kind of laughter that was almost gloating. She confirmed it, that even with her successful restaurant, she was still whoring.

"Isn't that restaurant enough? Have you become so greedy that even with a business that is already making money, you still go into this?"

She jabbed a finger at me. "You really don't understand," her voice leaped. "What difference does it make now if I continued or stopped? People will always say, there goes the woman who made a lot of money from that Southeast Asian leader. She now runs a restaurant so men can see her on display and proposition her right there. So, why then shouldn't I make the most of it?"

Her logic escaped me. I loved her but now I loathed her as well. I decided not to see her again, to leave her to Andrew Meadows and the wrath of heaven. In the office, I had all calls screened and if it was she who called and she did that every day, I was out, in a conference or in Baguio. I did not take calls in the apartment.

It was a miserable, pain-wracked withdrawal.

I had read about alcoholics being wrenched away from the bottle and dried up, how addicts underwent agony after a day without their drugs. I now understood the anguish I had to go through was not so much for my salvation but for hers. I hoped she would get married properly so that she would have a new life, something I could never give her.

The tortured days turned into a week, then two weeks. One evening I jogged needlessly longer than usual at the Luneta, then went to the Sultan in Mabini for a good rub-down. I could hardly keep my eyes open when I reached the apartment.

I did not even remove my jogging shoes; I fell forward on my bed and promptly went to sleep.

The loud banging on the door woke me up. Still sleepy, I staggered to the door. It was the guard downstairs and with him was Ermi. I thanked him but even before I could ask Ermi what brought her to Mabini at this time of night, she had pushed me back to the room.

In the soft light of the lamp in the foyer, her face was ashen and the corners of her mouth curled in anger. "Roly," she cried. "What are you trying to do?"

I had not thought that my avoiding her, my silence really mattered to her. I shook my head. "I cannot hurt you," I said. "If I do, as I have always said, it is not intentional."

"Then, what do you call this? Keeping away from me as if I were a leper? Your office does not give you my calls and look!" She picked up the phone which was disconnected. "You are doing this intentionally. What have I done to you that you should hate me?"

"I want you to have a good life, a good marriage—all the things this little daddy cannot give. Andy has everything."

She rushed to me, embraced me. "Tonight," her voice was pleading, "let me stay with you. Please . . ."

I pushed her gently away, looked into her distraught face. "I don't have three thousand pesos."

"Stop it!" I was sure her scream carried through the door and across the hall. "Don't insult me anymore. Can't you see what you have done? Are you that blind and selfish?"

I shook my head.

"You condemn me, you look down on me. I am dirt to you. But what wrong have I done, Roly? Have I ever stolen from anyone like those big people whom you know and serve? It is them you should hate and fight—and they are everywhere, robbing the people, self-righteous, honored in the newspapers. I have—"

She did not continue; her eyes suddenly had a blank stare; she swayed and I rushed to her before she could fall.

Her body was rigid now, her arms were cold and I carried her to the bedroom, remembering what she said about going into hysteria. I rushed to the kitchen and got some ice cubes then returned to her, prostrate on my bed. I pressed the ice cubes to her face and slapped her hard once, twice. She finally stirred and when she opened her eyes, it would seem as if a great weight was finally lifted off me and I could breathe the good air again.

She looked at me bending over her and I kissed her mumbling senselessly, "Forgive me, forgive me . . ." She raised her arms in an embrace, her heart thumping against my chest. I held her tightly now and thanked God for this gift of love.

FOUR

Long afterwards, I lay awake, viewing the rubble of my resolution and how, in the end, I was not more durable or steadfast. It was not that I regretted this union—poignant, quivering in its intensity. Though she never asked me for the money that I should have paid her or even made the slightest hint of it, still, it was in my mind like some fishbone stuck in the throat, at times painful, at times unnoticed but still there. I recalled what she had told me about the men who had showered her with costly gifts. "They all wanted me to fall for them," she said with coldblooded detachment, "so that they could have me for free."

I had enough experience to realize that there was no difference really between commercial sex and what was consummated with a loved one—the orgasm was the same. Still, there was more meaning, more "soul" to a relationship nurtured with affection, familiarity, and sometimes, communion. It was this that I found with Ermi.

I asked her once if she did not feel squeamish with older men and she had said, only if they were not good to her—an ambiguous reply, and I wondered about the depth of her feelings for me which she had kept to herself. I did not expect anything from her, yet I ached to know, to be told that she thought of me a little. I also imagined something pure about my love—an essence, a distillation and now, I was worried that it had been sullied not so much by the physical deed itself but because I needed to know more than ever the answers to the unspoken questions about her sincerity.

We talked till dawn stole through the windows, gleamed on the blue drapes and I could trace the fine contour of her face, the beautiful rise of her breasts. We talked about inchoate feelings, the future that did not hold much. She also admitted that she rarely had an orgasm, no matter how handsome the man, no matter how virile. She said she would not go out again to sell her favors, that although I would not believe her, she had to do this now for herself.

She came to Mabini almost every night after that and sometimes she would stay till morning. One early dawn, we woke up to fire engines wailing in the rain-drenched street below and looking out of the window, we saw our district turning red; the Filipinas Hotel was burning, the flames leaping up the starless sky. Many who were trapped in the building died of asphyxiation. Some jumped out of their windows, some into the pool below. Those who fell into the pool were saved, but many could not jump that far and their battered bodies lined the pool edge. Many of those who died were companions of tourists for the night and about them little was known. Who would miss five dozen prostitutes? They would be nothing but statistics and their relatives might not even go to the authorities to claim their bodies or even identify them.

I would take her out for breakfast at Taza de Oro and on the way, we would meet them—the girls with oversized handbags coming out of the Aurelio, the Bay View and the other hotels in the area where they had spent the night. They would wait for taxis at the hotel fronts, their Japanese companions waving good-bye to them. Pedro at the Taza soon knew what she always ordered, waffles with bacon and a slice of papaya.

Sometimes, she would decide to return to Cubao past midnight and I would drive her there, wait in the car while she fumbled at the gate with her keys. I did not leave till she was safely inside.

I told her of what I learned in one of my trips to Bangkok: how girls from a barren part of that country—the Northeast—went to Bangkok to sell themselves and once they had earned enough money, they would return home to get married, raise a family.

"There is no stigma to them," I said.

"I wish I were Thai," she said quietly.

She wanted a baby but was afraid she would not be able to have one anymore. "I will not mind what people will say. I will love him so much he will never regret that I was his mother . . ."

I asked her if she had such regrets and she told me that all she remembered of her childhood were those days in the orphanage in Quezon City where she gew up. I wanted to know more but she clammed up.

We were in my apartment drinking the coffee that she had brewed that morning. Outside, Ermita was beginning to stir; already the jeepneys were snorting down below the window and farther up the bay, the sun was glinting on the calm, glasslike sea.

"If it is a boy, you will be the godfather."

"I'd rather be the father," I said, wondering if there was any man lurking in the shadows about whom I did not know. It had been that way, my mind riled by questions, by doubts. How would one distinguish, for instance, the sincerity of her embrace? She had told me she had faked it many times with her men so how different then was it with me? I wanted to exact from her the promise that she would never leave me although I knew that she would someday. How does one measure truth? There was only one way by which I would be able to know. And I hesitated to tell her for fear that, just by telling her, I would lose her.

"I know some girls in Camarin," she said. "At the opening of the school year, or when their children get sick, they don't know what to do."

"I know what you mean," I said. "This apartment, or this district, is not even the place to rear children. But one thing sure, I will not run away from my responsibilities. I can set up a trust fund for him so that when he gows up, he will not be in want."

"Replay. That is an old tune," she said, pinching my arm.

"But it is still true."

"Think of your own circle, your friends. Oh, I know you mean it and you can live with what I am. But they will sneer at you, your settling down after all these years with a prostitute from Camarin. Do you think you can endure that? And if we go out to some dinner and there is a man, or two men, whom I know, how would you take it?"

I could not answer. It had not occurred to me that she would put it that way, so neatly, so clearly.

"Maybe," I said, "we can go somewhere and live by ourselves."

"And how long can that be? We cannot really run away." I thought that if she were constantly with me, my anxieties would be banished, that her presence would be the balm to ease my mind and I would finally settle into comfortable domesticity. But the new relationship was soon battered and awry. We were both to blame, I guess—she for her volatile temper and hypersensitivity to things I said, and me for my candor and openness. There were now bickerings between us, sometimes bitter and long-drawn. It was better if I kept my mouth taped, afraid that I would say something that would make her cross.

Now her presence seemed unreal; when she was gone, it would seem as if she had not been with me at all. There was no lingering trace of her although I always remembered what she said. I was so insecure with her, I was afraid she would even walk out on me in the middle of the night when she was in one of her unexplainable moods.

During one quarrel I was so exasperated with her tempestuousness, I told her perhaps it was best if she became an actress. We had driven sullenly to Cubao and even when she reached her gate, there was none of the joyous reconciliation that I had expected. I spent the night in turmoil, my chest tightened like a vise, and sleep would not come. I had to see her the following day, wait humbly at her gate till she came out.

Her new belligerence confounded me; I suspected that she did this so that she could dominate me and I took pains explaining to her that our relationship should not be one of superiority or inferiority; I had no intention of changing her personality, I took her for what she was. But even a remark like this was enough to send her into a dark and sulking mood.

Often, in those anxious moments of silence, I raked the past and asked myself what wrong I had done. I searched my conscience—the innermost recesses of myself—and there was nothing I could remember which I did wrong. There was one evening when she simply said it was time for goodbye. She did not want to see me anymore. I was caressing her face when she drew away. I was amassing memories, and God, many of them were bitter. I know that whatever it was I had told her, I was just being myself, I was expressing my nagging fears and nothing else. I concluded then that she was either playing with me or had finally gotten tired because I had nothing to give, nothing but this shriveled self.

We rarely talked about Andrew Meadows now. I knew he would soon leave. Then, by early April, she called and said she wanted me to visit her in Cubao. It was the first time she would let me in, the first man, she said, whom she had ever invited there. We were going to be alone, she was going to send her "family" out to see a movie or to shop at Ali Mall nearby.

She met me gravely at the gate and when a maid lingered, she told her briskly to go out to the garden and water the palmettos, among them, I am sure, the palmetto I had bought for her in Calamba. She was pale and drawn and her eyes seemed glazed. She led me to her house. Though not large it was tastefully decorated. I was happily surprised to see myself everywhere, the knickknacks I had given her, the lacquered trays, the flower vases, the art books. She led me to her bedroom and for a moment, I thought we would make love.

"I am sorry that I had to get you out of your office in the middle of the afternoon," she said. "But I want you to know—to be the first to know that I have made a decision."

I thought she had finally decided to live with me.

"I am going to marry Andy," she said.

The news sank into me with such truculence, my knees felt weak and a deadening sense of loss engulfed me. I had felt this sorrow only once before, when Lydia and the children left me.

I could not speak.

"It is for the best, Roly," she said. "For both of us. For you . . . and your morality. It will mean that you are finally free of me. Can't you see? For me, it will be a beginning . . ."

"We must live with the past," I said, suppressing the tremor in my voice.

"I know," she said. "And we must also forget it. Andy wants to take me to America, make a home for him and raise his children. I saw a gynecologist last week. He said I could still bear half a dozen children if I wanted to. And that is what I will do. I will raise them in a happy home and will love them all I can . . ."

I pressed her hand. I didn't want to but I understood.

I remembered when she asked me if she looked like a prostitute and how I felt then, how I wanted to be one with her.

"I wish you the best . . ." I said, even as tears blurred my eyes. But she did not see them for she embraced me then and started to cry, her heart thrashing against my chest. It was the last time I would hold her.

"All the men I had, the boyfriend-boyfriends, I never felt anything for them. I don't love Andy, Roly. But perhaps, in time, I will. It was you all the time, the first . . ."

I tried to push her away, to look at the precious face but she would not let me. My cheeks were soon wet with her crying.

"Can you imagine how long it has been?" she asked. "So now, I know what love is. When you said you wanted a relationship that was not plastic, I did not understand. I do now. I have never apologized to any man. Now, I will say to you—" she kissed me softly—"please forgive me . . ."

Leaving Cubao at dusk, the heat of April melting my bones, I really had nowhere to go. I was happy for Ermi. Perhaps, this is what love has always been, whether it is for a woman or for a cause—the readiness to give and not ask for anything in return, the unquestioning willingness to lose everytlung, even if that loss is something as precious as life itself.

"What is death?" she had once asked. "You die once and you will not die again . . ."

Remembering this, I know how it would be for me. I would return to the old apartment in Mabini and if I could not sleep, I would probably walk over to Camarin. Ralph, the pianist had retired; a son had taken him back to Agusan. Where the piano used to stand they have set up a booth for their stereo system. The bar had deteriorated since Didi migrated to the United States and they no longer had Jack Daniels black. I would probably order a beer and squid roasted in that open grill, then watch Gloria finish her routine. She is buxom like a Rubens girl, she gyrates her hips in a naughty, lascivious way.

After Camarin, I would go to the Luneta and get a bit of salt air in my lungs. I would wait for the night to deepen then return to my apartment and lie down on that wide and empty bed. I would imagine Ermi as it was the night she stormed in. I can still see her even now bending over me, her hair a tumble on my face, her breath warm and sweet. But did she really care? I had asked her to be kind when the moment for my execution came, that she make it swift. I will always languish in her final judgment about how I sold myself. She was right, of course, but it was not just myself that I had sold. And though I will not admit it to anyone, ever, I know that I sold my country, too—I, Rolando Cruz, former guerrilla officer, historian. What have I done to rationalize this treason? They used me—the gnomes of Wall Street and Marunouchi. I did their bidding willingly, eagerly, for I wanted a life that would not be marred by the early hunger that I had known. I had gotten more than food, but now, it was not only Ermi whom I had lost. What will she take of me from this Ermita that had been my perdition and her beginning? I don't even have her picture. And knowing that what should be must be, I will probably be wracked by this pain which not even morphine can allay, and when it will finally become intolerable, I will probably go to the compartment under my bookshelf, take out the old forty-five kept from my days in Kiangan, then level it at my head.

Baguio, May 29, 1980.

PLATINUM

ONE

It is difficult for me to relate this story because it concerns a woman for whom I have always had the deepest affection. Also because it concerns me and the dilemmas that I had to face, not in our relationship, but in the very probing questions she had raised, not so much by what she asked as by the way she had lived.

I am convinced that I loved her as I had never loved anyone. If I did leave my easy life to be with her in the end as I told her I would, it was because of her. I know now that she was right and yet, I have not really changed. Is it because I am a coward? Too much a creature of habit, of comfort? Or—and I don't want to answer this question—did I really love her enough?

Every day, I go through the numbing monotony, doing what I have been doing for the last six years. I have prospered by any measure in spite of inflation, the energy crisis, and all those pernicious dislocations that threatened business under martial law. And still I persist although no longer believing in what I am doing. Why then? For the family tradition? Out of momentum or plain, cussed stubbornness?

But I am young and there is time ahead.

Is it because I don't want to stake my life in a venture which may not bring forth the justice Malu had searched for? I don't want to think anymore. My mind is in turmoil and I wish Malu were here to confirm me.

I met Malu—short for Maria Luisa—in my senior year when I was contributing to the college journal. I was majoring in business and economics, but I had dabbled in sociology. Thinking about it now, Malu must have regarded me as an incorrigible rightist. I was about to leave the office of Professor Galvez, having submitted a twenty-page manuscript on the multinational corporations and how they were plundering Mindanao, when she came in.

She was tall—almost as tall as I—very fair, and slim. Her hair was neatly combed, hanging loose over her shoulders. She did not have a bit of makeup. But even without cosmetics, her face seemed aglow—that was the first thing one noticed about Malu. She had high cheekbones, full lips, and eyes that shone. Her chest was almost flat, and a fine down covered her arms.

Professor Galvez, who was the journal's editor, attended to her at once. "Ah, Malu, I suppose you've already finished the piece. About time we had something spiritually lifting in this arid little journal."

Her face was mobile; she was plainly peeved.

"Your article on faith healing and spirits," Professor Galvez went on blithely, "should really make the next issue more interesting."

"That is what I came to tell you, sir." Her voice was mellow. "I'm hesitant about it. I wrote it in the first person and it doesn't have the objectivity you demand."

Professor Galvez had a Ph.D. in clinical psychology. He was also an excellent writer. In his late forties, his hair had turned prematurely gray and he looked venerable. "Well, isn't that the best way to handle something that cannot be explained in the usual scholarly fashion? But we can always break gound the way Carlos Castañeda does."

Again, the displeasure on her face which the professor missed entirely.

We went out together. I wanted to know her more and what she was doing. She was free the rest of the morning so we went to the cafeteria for coffee.

I was pretentious then, going on pompous. I believed in economic nationalism and was researching the policies of government that were inimical to our interests . It was 1970 and though I did not agree with the student demonstrators and their lofty, radical slogans, I sympathized with their objectives. Malu told me later that I was just expressing the "constipated" view of the nationalist bourgeoisie which wanted the whole cake for itself.

She listened patiently nonetheless to how I was gappling with such weighty subjects as history, progress, and alienation. Thinking back, had Malu been plain, I would not have been interested in her or what she was doing. Faith healing was old news to me, although I wasn't one to go around writing about spirits.

"It is not that he lacks empathy, because he is good," she said, still irritated by Professor Galvez's remarks which, she said, were patronizing. "He is less a Filipino—like all the rest who have gone to the United States and brought back all those inappropriate ideas about research and methodology. Look, all over the country, in spite of our science and our Christianity, a belief in the world of the spirit persists. This world is open to everyone who wants to enter it. Nothing exotic or mysterious. All of us have experienced an inkling, a premonition. Extrasensory perception they call it now. The early Christians were mystics. And Saint Theresa of Avila levitated. The Bible is full of miracles—and why not? Is mysticism Christian when even Christians hardly believe in it anymore? Those who flock to Baclaran or Quiapo praying to those images for favors, that's not mysticism. It is just simple human need, a natural reaching out to the supernatural . . ."

I liked the way she explained it. I knew how right she was. In my senior year in high school, I was in the library one afternoon when I distinctly heard Father's voice. I turned, expecting to see him. But there was no one. As a matter of fact, I was alone except for the clerks at the far end.

I was very disturbed and since it was already late in the day and I had no more classes, I decided to go home instead of playing basketball. Only the maids were in; Mother had rushed to the hospital. Father had had a heart attack and had died at about the same time I heard his voice.

"That is not unusual," Malu said. "It has been documented. The air is charged with energy, the spirits of people, and sometimes, in cases of great urgency, contact is made."

The semester was about over; it was a faultless October morning and the sun shone brilliant on the campus, washing the gass and the cream-colored buildings with dazzling light. She did not want to linger in the cafeteria so we crossed the street to the library and beyond it to this huge acacia tree—perhaps the biggest in the entire campus. She liked its cool shade and we were to meet again and again beneath it.

I was flattered that she had read my article listing the economic imperatives of nationalism. She said it was well argued, but then she added that it lacked social purpose. What was nationalism *for*? What did it mean to the lower classes, to those who worked the land?

So her interests were also in the here and now. Aside from her involvement with ESP and spirits, she turned out to be a political activist.

We had barely seated ourselves on a protruding root of the tree when she asked if I had joined any of the student demonstrations that were sweeping the city. I had not bothered with them. With a touch of melancholy, she said, "I think you're a dilettante . . . engrossed with the veneer and not with the pith."

I reminded her about what a Frenchman once said: if one is not a communist when one is eighteen, he has no heart;

but if he is still a communist when he is forty, he has no head. She retorted that I was neither eighteen nor forty—so what did that make me? And then she railed against the inequities that surrounded us, this girl who lived in an exclusive Makati village, who went to an expensive school. She was going to teach me, she said with some levity, what social awareness was.

Malu was majoring in clinical psychology and was, I am sure, never short of subjects. I suppose that she considered me one, given the manner she asked questions. Often she would be quiet as if my answers were being studied and fitted into her equations. She had a tendency to be patronizing like Professor Galvez. She called me "Teng-ga," meaning lead, which could have easily been "Tanga," meaning stupid. I was ponderous, capable of thought, but when all was said, the profundity was without value. I was not concerned with the kind of justice that could only be brought about by a mass movement.

At first, I resented the nickname. I decided to give her one in kind.

"I know myself, " I said. "And the man who knows himself is not only secure but wise."

"But there are things you don't know about yourself," she insisted. "And knowing oneself is not being profound. It is being conceited."

"And you are not?"

"I don't think I am the center of the universe."

"I suppose you consider yourself some sort of precious metal then. Like gold."

She shook her head. "I am not expensive."

"But you are," I said. "With your ideas, who is the man who can afford to love you? Imagine what you will do to his psyche, if not his wallet."

As if on impulse, she stretched out her hand and held mine.

"And you think you're heavy, too," I said.

I remembered my parents' wedding rings—they were heavy and they looked plain, like silver, or even lead, but they were expensive. "Platinum. That's what you think you are. I will call you Plat."

"Male revenge!" she exclaimed. "And I am thin, my breasts are no bigger than *kalamansi*!"

Her candor touched me. "But their smallness cannot diminish your beauty, Plat. And I would like to make them grow."

"Into pomelos." She laughed.

I wanted to take her home the next afternoon so that I could meet her parents, but she demurred. She guessed what I had in mind. "You are so square," she said, crinkling her nose as if some bad odor assailed her. "You would like to pay court in the traditional way and ask Father for my hand. You should work in our house then, chop firewood, draw water from the well. After all these sacrifices, are you sure you will have a virgin?" She was putting it lightly, but then she came close and breathed into my face. "But I like the way you are doing it."

She would not give me her address. This I found out soon enough from the registrar's office where I had a friend. I went there on a Sunday morning and since her house was in Dasmariñas Village, I was not surprised that it was grand. Unlike most of the houses in this expensive Makati area, it was done in the old colonial style—red-tile roof, thick adobe walls, intricate ironwork on the sash windows and balustrades, and a heavy gate of solid molave with iron braces and filigrees. I also realized why she did not want me to visit her—this girl who always rode in buses and jeepneys, who dressed in T-shirt and faded jeans and formless *katsa*—a fabric similar to cheesecloth—blouses; she was trying to live down the fact that she was rich.

"But in the beginning we were not," she explained.

My visit had surprised her, but she had asked me in. We proceeded to the patio that overlooked a wide, well-groomed garden, and she served me coffee and the chocolate cake her mother had baked.

"It was all my father's doing. He is a good businessman. He had this land in Bataan which later became very expensive property. He is a genius in real estate—no one can steal him blind . . ."

It was meant to be a pun of sorts. Her father was tortured by the Japanese during the war and had lost his sight. He had given Malu as a child a sense of inferiority; she was particularly annoyed when her classmates called him "Antiojos" because of the dark glasses he always wore, even on that evening when she graduated (as valedictorian) in grade school. She went with him on trips, describing places and people, reading the papers to him. She had become adept at description and at intuition by being his perceptive eyes.

I felt that she reluctantly brought me up to the house afterwards because she did not want me to see its rich interior. But I wanted to meet her father, this man who had taught her vision and forebearance. He sat before a TV set, listening to a documentary on Japanese culture. When we entered the room, he turned to the sound of our entry. His eyes were unblinking, glimpsed through the dark glasses. He extended his hand and I grasped it. His grip was strong and warm. Malu was right—if I did not know, I would have thought he was not blind at all. "So, at last" he turned to her. "You have brought a young man home. I suppose it is serious then."

Malu pinched my arm. "Yes, sir," I said, not minding her.

"Well, Malu has one more year in college. I suppose both of you can wait."

Malu was glaring at me even as I said, "Hardly, sir."

There was exuberant closeness in the family. Malu was the youngest and was the favorite. She had a way with almost anyone and was headstrong. I knew they accepted me when her father told me to forgive Malu's vaulting enthusiasms. And boys, it seemed, were not one of them. He tolerated her politics; she was doing, he said, what he would do were he young again.

The audience over, Malu took me to the garden.

Again, the familiar cliches about the working class, the blighted rural areas.

"But do you really know how it is over there? In the most depressed parts of the country?" I questioned the factual basis of her judgments. "You have never lived on a farm," I said, badgering her.

"Do you know how I can be in one?" she asked. "I will bring a team—all girls, at least a dozen of us."

Uncle Bert had this farm in Albay, but if they stayed with him, they would be comfortable. I asked him to arrange for the "education" of a dozen *colegialas,* that they be exposed to the worst conditions in Bicol. Uncle Bert laughed and said he would see to that.

After the semestral break, she returned from Albay sunburned, her hands blistered. But there was a radiance in her face. They had paid economy fare at Tutuban station. They did not bring any food because they thought they would have their meals in the first-class restaurant on the train. They were herded into a dusty coach which pitched and loped when they were finally on the way. Vegetables and crates were piled on the corridors and platforms. There was no place for them to sit except on the crates. They got hungry and there was no restaurant in third class.

Some passengers offered them their food—cold chunks of rice with pieces of dried fish wrapped in banana leaves. They bought additional food from vendors in the stations.

The farm she was assigned to was at the foot of a mountain, and isolated. Many days she felt she would simply go mad. She would wander beyond the house and shout her lungs dry just so she could hear herself. After mundane conversations with the family, she had no one to talk with, nothing to read. She did not bring a novel, not even a writing pad, and the family did not have a transistor radio. There was no flush toilet and worse, she forgot to bring toilet paper.

The family's lack of interest in politics of the kind she believed in did not faze her; she had met the same skepticism and even suspicion in the slum families of Tondo when she started teach-ins. She had to talk with them in terms of their needs, what they could relate to in their daily lives—why prices of copra were low, who made the money in the trade, and why they worked so hard and yet earned so little.

She was amazed at their endurance. They would climb the foothills to gather coconuts then bring them to the yard where they were husked. The two youngsters in the family who were not even in their teens carried four coconuts each and she carried only two. By the time she reached the top of the hill, she was so tired and breathless from crawling on her knees and hands, while her young companions would still be bouncing ahead of her. She also helped in the harvesting in the valley. Bent over in the field, she could only work briefly in the morning when it was not too hot. She would be drenched with sweat, she itched horribly, and her back ached so much she thought it would break.

She had brought some canned food and was sure the family fed her with the best they could afford. She did not want to appear conspicuous so she brought her oldest clothes. There was a funeral in the village, but even with her rags, she was the best dressed.

Still, she was when she returned home, as I said, radiant.

TWO

It was not my intention to wean Malu from her politics, just see to it that she saw the other side, that progress was not a result of a class war, that motivation was important, and that as a student of psychology, she should recognize this.

I saw her almost daily during lunch when school started again if she was not in the slums or in demonstrations at the American embassy and Malacañang. I was going to graduate in a few months and had already started working in the family business. Perhaps it sounded flippant when I asked if she was now ready, after all her experiences, to move out of Dasmariñas and lead the revolution.

She was not usually given to flare-ups, but this time, she all but screamed, "Damn your money! How much do you pay your workers?"

I did not let that pass. I asked if she ever understood why so many generations stayed on in Tondo which had been there in Bonifacio's time, and even earlier. "They are lazy, they lack initiative," I told her. "You can love humanity—but it will not change."

"And why should they not be lazy?" she flung back. "This is the whole debilitating effect of colonialism. They work so hard and still don't make enough. Or eat enough."

"In our furniture factory," I said, "there is a lot of absenteeism after payday. What do they do? They get drunk and don't report for work for three days. They don't save. I can go through a long list."

"But not in the farms where your uncle sent us."

"They are not his farms. All of us, we give justice to our workers."

"They work very hard," she went on. "Without rest, and when all is done, there is still very little for them." Then she challenged me. "I bet you have never been in a slum, you have never been inside a poor man's house, in Tondo or anywhere."

She trapped me, all right, and that very afternoon, it was my turn. We drove to Barrio Magsaysay where her group was organizing action teams.

We parked in the bay boulevard because we could not get through the maze of alleys. It was late November, the rains had paused; otherwise, as she explained it, we would have to wear boots because the alleys became rivulets of fetid mud. When we got there, what disturbed me really was not the sorry construction, the pigsty atmosphere—it was the eagerness, the dedication on her face as we entered this misshapen world of people who greeted her with warmth.

She introduced me to Charlie—a frail boy of fifteen who looked much older, and like all youths in the slum, he had dirty skin and bad teeth. He was in faded shorts and his rubber slippers were about to break apart. Wherever we went, he followed. He adored Malu and for a while, I was jealous.

"He is the brightest boy in the Barrio," she said, enthusiastically. He had organized the youngsters and got them to clean the alleys, keep order. He was out of school; he would have been a high school junior had he enrolled, but his tuition money went to the hospital when his father fell ill. He helped at a stall in Divisoria, got three pesos a day plus some leftover, wilted vegetables.

There were many things that Malu could have done for them but she felt they must do a lot for themselves and I agreed. Still I knew that someday, if it had not already happened, they would possess her and I did not want that. I coveted her.

It was late afternoon when we left the Barrio. We went to the Hilton. I had thought of walking around the Luneta but she was hungry.

We sat together in the coffee shop and I held her hand under the table. Her closeness was intoxicating, an invitation; I was now sure she had some affection for me. I relished that Sunday morning when I visited her, warmed to the memory of her pinching me when I told her father how serious my intentions were. I just loved looking at her, the sinuous line of her jaw, those eyes, expressive of joy and yet seeing sorrow everywhere. I loved listening to her even when she was like some broken record repeating the same phrases about the oppression of the poor which, really, no single person could change for as long as we lived within the iron logic of capitalism.

"I am miserable, Teng-ga," she said, pressing my hand. "I can't find peace of mind. Oh, no, not the spiritual kind. It seems as if I'm at ease only when I am trying to help people."

She moved closer. I desired her then, imagined her naked under me, crushing those lips in a kiss. Looking at her, composed and serene, I wondered how she would look in surrender, her self-assurance completely sundered.

I did something stupid that day which, as it turned out, was a revelation not only about myself but about her. We had finished our hamburgers. The late afternoon was untarnished and driving along the boulevard, the smell of the sea wafting into the car, she sat close to me, silent, as if her mind were far away. Soon, it would be dark. As we turned left through Cuneta to get to Makati, the motels lined up on both sides on the narrow road.

"Let's go into one," I said, and before she could object, I had turned left to an entrance. She tugged at my sleeve briefly as if to stop me, but it was too late. I swung the car to an open garage which one of the boys who had risen from a bench pointed to.

I had expected her to object, perhaps just a little. She looked at me, shaking her head, then she rolled up the window and together, we went up the stairs. It was obviously her first time in a motel and now, she was all curiosity as she studied the room, the huge mirrors that surrounded the wide bed, the knobs that controlled the red lights and the piped-in music. When the buzzer rang and the boy came, she went out to the anteroom and watched me sign the smudged register with a fictitious name.

After the boy had gone, she sat on the wide bed, looked disapprovingly at me, and asked, "Are you going to rape me?"

I shook my head. "I am not going to do anything you don't want. "

"I am glad you said that," she said, "because I'm not ready for this. Oh, I know that by the time you are a junior in the university, you are no longer supposed to be a virgin. But I still am—whatever you may think of my manners."

"And you're proud of holding on to it?"

"Maybe, but that is not the reason. I would like to give it to someone I really care for."

I do not know of her intention but what she said dampened my ardor.

"I suppose I am not the first girl you brought to a motel?"

"No," I said with some honesty.

"I am getting to like you," she said with a slight laugh. "And who knows . . ." she stood up, came to me, and kissed my cheek. I flung my arms around her, kissed the lobes of her ears, felt her body warm and close, her silky thighs. But she was like a block of wood. I let her go.

"You're a tease," I said. "You lead me on and let me think . . ."

"I am not a tease," her voice rose. "Can't you see that I like you, but not enough to engage in simple fornication? That is what you want—and if you love me, then you know that love is more than that."

"Shit," I said, turning. "Even the church dissolves a marriage if it is not consummated. Spiritual love—that is foolish, for nuns. And even nuns have physical needs. Don't you realize that I want to marry you?"

"Thank you for the nice thought." Her tone changed immediately. She shucked off her shoes, then lay down. "Come," she said. "Let's not waste this bed and all these mirrors. Let us just talk."

I could not help but laugh. Desire had really cooled. I lay beside her and gazed at the mirror in the ceiling, at the two of us, fully clothed.

"No one would believe this," I said. Then I asked her what it was that she really wanted to do.

"To be alive," she said quietly. "To see that time is not wasted. I don't want to gow old without having lived usefully."

"Loving is living," I said. "So I love you and in loving you I *am* alive." I lay still, her hand warm and soft in mine, the blisters from Albay already gone. "But suppose I died tomorrow; what is it that you will remember of me?"

She turned on her side and pressed her hand quickly to my mouth. "Don't talk like this. As if you always look at the dark side of things."

"There can be a car accident tomorrow. Or a building may collapse on me. These we cannot foresee. Living is always risking."

She lay back. Even when we did not speak, I could feel myself flow out to her in calm, blue waves. We reminisced about ourselves, her childhood, those days when she had been so self-conscious with her father and how, by that experience, she had learned to use her eyes better and see beneath the patina, the superficiality of appearances and of speech. It was deeds that mattered.

I reiterated; I would soon be through with school and would then take on more duties in our business. It was time to get married.

And that was when she said we could just live together and find out if we were compatible so that, afterwards, if we weren't, or if we outgrew each other, we could always part and still be friends.

I was shocked. She was a modern, liberated woman, but I did not know she thought so lightly of the institution of marriage.

"You are fooling, Plat."

"No," she said amiably. "Marriage is a lifetime commitment and that is what I want to make when I am sure."

The telephone jangled. The clerk said our "short time" was up. Four hours! Time had gone so fast, it was almost midnight. I wanted to stay longer since there were many things still unsaid, many questions unasked.

We put on our shoes. She brushed her hair and straightened her blouse. I went behind her and encircled her waist. Turning to me, she kissed me again lightly, this time on the lips.

"So, at least," she whispered, "you will not say that nothing happened."

We drove to Dasmariñas hardly talking. Her mother opened the door saying, "Hurry, your father needs you."

I was uneasy, wondering what scolding she would get.

Her mother asked me to stay for a cup of coffee. She was a handsome woman in her fifties, without the matronly bulge of most women her age. In her blue housedress, there was a patrician quality about her, and her eyes, like Malu's, were alive. Look at a girl's mother, I remember reading, and this is how the daughter will look.

I asked permission to leave, but Malu returned to the living room and told me to wait, her father wanted to talk with me.

"I told him we went to a motel," she said, laughing.

Her mother must have seen me blush. She smiled at my discomfiture and said Malu was always making those risque jokes. But she is a good girl, she assured me.

"I know that, Ma'am" I said.

She left for the kitchen and returned with the coffee and a piece of chocolate cake.

"She is giving her father a head massage," she explained. "He is not feeling well."

"I did not know she was also a masseuse."

"Not really," she explained. "She just lays her hand on her father's brow then prays."

I wanted to know more, but by then Malu came out and said I should talk with her father. I was nervous—did she *really* tell him we went to a motel? And would he tell me now never again to come to this house?

She led me across the wide expanse of carpet and upholstered furniture and all that "burgis crockery" as she described it, to the library. By an old writing desk with several tape recorders, Malu's father sat on an overstuffed leather easy chair. His dark glasses were not on and when he looked at me, his eyes had that blank, unseeing stare. He must have felt that I was standing for he said, "Please sit down," pointing to the rattan chair before him.

He asked if I was served something and when he was

assured that I was, he sighed, "I had this headache again and Malu is the only one who can relieve me of it."

"She is a wonderful girl, sir."

He nodded. "She has special gifts. She is the brightest of my children. I know her values are right. She tells me about those teach-ins, those demonstrations, the idealism of it all. I worry about her, her safety, her well-being. If she were only a boy—do you understand what I am trying to say?"

"Yes, sir."

"Do you believe in what she is doing?"

"Not all the way, sir," I said. "Neither demonstrations nor guns will do away with the injustice around us. Education will—I told her that."

He slapped his thigh as if he agreed, drew his chest in and breathed deeply. He was past sixty, but there was still stamina in him. "But how can I dissuade her? I believe in her goals, too, and that is why I am worried. But I'm glad that you are rooted in solid ground and you can be some sort of anchor to . . . reason and sanity. Now, let me tell you something you don't know. She is also a *spiritista.* Do you know what that is?"

"Yes, sir. She let me read a paper she wrote which she did not want published."

He shook his head, sadly. "Since 1949—nothing but darkness. Many specialists, even in Europe, have seen me. Do you understand? I was prepared for a life of darkness. I have even forgiven the Japanese for it. I have adjusted to it, although I miss many things. The shape of trees, of houses, the colors . . . and Malu—my dear child! I have never seen her. If only I could! Sometimes, I touch her face, imagining how she looks. She always tells me she is ugly."

"No, sir," I said quickly. "She is the prettiest girl I know. Her eyes, her cheeks . . ." I was gushing and pitying him at the same time. And I was glad that I could see her and hoped to God that I would know her far better, know the grace that suffused her personality.

"You love her?"

"Very much, sir."

"We all love her," he said. "But I have a feeling that we will lose her."

"Oh, no!"

The sightless eyes locked with mine. "You may not know it, but when she became a *spiritista* two years ago . . . Oh—I never found out how she got into it and she has not told me yet. During this last year that she began ministering to me, touching my eyes, praying for me . . . I could not believe it at first. After all those years of total darkness. But now, I can tell when it is daylight. The reds come flooding into my eyes. Do you know what this means? For a man who knew nothing but night for more than twenty years? I have hope again. And now, when I sit in front of a window, when people pass in front of me, I see shadows. Shadows!"

Malu came to the acacia after her last class; she wore the same old jeans and loose blouse—they were her uniform. She shared with me the chocolate cake her mother had baked and when we were finished, I asked about the *spiritistas* in Navotas.

"And why are you so interested in them all of a sudden?"

"I want to find out what is in them that attracts you. What are you really looking for? What do you want?"

"Hey!" She playfully shoved a fist into my stomach. "One at a time. I am no computer. What do you want me to be?"

"My wife," I said immediately. "I want you to raise my children, to keep house, help me be what I want to be . . ."

"How conventional," she sighed. "The woman's place is in the home."

"It is a major responsibility, Plat. No small matter."

"I don't deny that," she said. "But it is like condemning a woman to prison."

"A home a prison? Do you want to be free like a bird? But even birds have nests."

"I know, but you asked what I want. I want peace."

"It is so abstract, Plat. It is like saying I want truth, beauty . . ."

"I want those, too, and they are not abstract."

"Tell me, are you uncomfortable in Dasmariñas Village?"

She did not speak. I had touched the root of it all. She turned to me and said evenly, "My father did not cheat anyone. He worked very hard all his life. My mother, too. I don't have to explain our kind of life."

"I am not asking you to," I said. "People deserve the fruits of their labor."

"That's what Father said. The only things I knew were parties, clothes. Oh, yes, Father told us about the poor, but I was protected from real knowledge. Then, when I was a junior in high school, I had a very good teacher in literature. She made us read Rizal, all those stories by our own writers that would waken us. We asked questions. She took us to the Philippine General Hospital and saw all those people in the corridors who were going to die because they had no money. I have been only to the best hospitals—the Makati Center, those in the United States. We read stories about the slums, so we visited—not Tondo—but Malibay in Pasay. And you know, what I used to spend for one dress—that was what one family needed to live on for three months! I was shocked. I felt guilty that I had so much, that I was comfortable and there are so many people who are not. And my teacher, when the nuns learned about what she was doing, they fired her. I really hated them for that."

"You cannot be Santa Claus," I said. "This is a job for government. Besides, the poor will always be with us."

"They are *people*!" she said emphatically. "That I cannot forget. I wanted to think only of myself, of the fun I used to have. I just couldn't anymore. And that was when I went into meditation. To ease my mind—not to run away or to seek some enlightenment. Don't you have mental or emotional problems at all?"

"Yes," I said. "Lots of them. But the one that gives me the most frustration—is you."

Her brows arched in mock surprise. "You trouble me a lot, too," she said. "We should meditate together then. I have my own mantra which is just like saying the rosary over and over."

"Om ni pad ni om . . ."

"Not that esoteric," she said. "What I want the world to have: love . . . light, love . . . light."

She said there must be a way the sick can be helped without going to fancy hospitals and buying those expensive medicines. Many of man's diseases were psychosomatic and most ailments could be cured by the human body itself. She went searching for faith healers, found most of them were fakes taking advantage of the ignorant, just as many specialists in medicine took advantage of their patients.

All these led her to the *spiritistas.*

"Can you take me to Navotas to see them?"

"So you can laugh at us, or look at us as if we were freaks?"

I told her then what her father had told me.

"I believe, Plat," I said simply.

. . .

We reached Barrio Santa Clara late in the day. It was not a long way from the boulevard that skirted the bay. We passed new housing areas that were being built on land that was once fish ponds. We turned right into a narrow, cemented street, the wooden houses intruding into the street itself. I drove slowly for people had spilled out into the street, loafing, taking in the late afternoon sun.

The chapel was within a compound of shoddy wooden frame houses and we parked in the driveway cluttered with laundry lines, empty fish baskets, and old lumber. Beyond the driveway, the chapel was just another decrepit building with an open foyer through which I could see no pews but an enclosure with several women and men. They greeted Malu warmly. She introduced me as her future husband and they beamed at me and shook my hand.

We did not stay with them; she led me out to one of the houses by the chapel, across an alley heaped with cooking pots, stacked firewood, and empty chicken coops. The whole place smelled of sweat and tired people. In the dim, almost sepulchral living room, a corpulent woman was stretched on an iron bed stacked with pillows that needed washing, her hair grayish and stringy. When she saw Malu, she half rose and grinned, baring a set of bad teeth stained with betel nut. Malu greeted her politely. She was the priestess, the leader of the congregation.

Dusk was now upon us. Back in the chapel, a single fluorescent tube in the nave was on and several candles in the altar with the image of Christ were lighted. They were all within the enclosure now. I sat just outside on one of the benches by the railing. They started with the national anthem, not the anthem sung in the schools with its exotic Tagalog. The melody was the same, but the words were simpler, more beautiful. The woman whom we had met in the house intoned a prayer first and all the members, not more than fifty and mostly women, stood silently. They were working-class people; their clothes were shabby, and their skins were dark with sun and toil. Now, their eyes closed, they started praying, Malu with them. After a while, many started to sway and tremble; the fat woman walked around, stood before each member, praying. I was transfixed, watching Malu. She had closed her eyes and her arms started to quiver. Each one spoke, not in unison but singly, in a Tagalog I could hardly understand, not the Tagalog of the sidewalk but the Tagalog of the poets. They thanked God and promised they would work for His glory. Then it was Malu's turn—the priestess was in front of her. Malu was in a deep trance and, perhaps, did not know what she was saying. Her voice was resonant, and her Tagalog was beautiful and frightening and I feared for her, for she said, "Dear God, Your poor and Your weak—Who will help them? When You said You gave us not peace but the sword, where now is the sword so that we may bring justice to Your people?"

For all her radical verbiage, Malu was not one to carry arms; she was scared of them and of military men. Her threshold for physical pain was low. She once suffered through a horrible toothache because she felt it was more torture to sit on a dentist's chair. Her childhood memories of her visit to one were indelible—the drill, it had seemed to her then, was going right through her tooth, into her being. I accompanied her to my dentist who was an excellent and understanding woman with a calm, soothing manner. Still, she paled visibly with the first shot of Novocain in her gums.

"How can you be a revolutionary when you cannot even visit a dentist without trembling? How will it be then when you get shot at? Or when you see blood?"

"You are no different—you're just like all of them," she said. "Did it ever occur to you that revolution is not just shooting and dying? It is also cooking, typing, keeping files, planning, teaching—and organizing."

I knew she was doing a lot of this and during the Christmas break that year, I saw her less, but I phoned every day. She was busy in the slums, worried that those driftwood houses would soon be bulldozed by the government.

"It is for the greater good, Plat," I said. "That place was meant for harbor facilities, for storehouses."

"But there is no place where they can be relocated," she said angrily. "And more than that, the government will not start any construction for two years. I know, I researched it."

I could not argue. Perhaps, I was just being jealous of Charlie who was now with her every day. I knew the slum needed not just simple housing but sewage disposal, garbage collection and a water system. Burned into my mind was that afternoon we went there, the pigpens that passed for homes, the unmistakable imprint of harsh living in the mottled skins of people, the big bellies of children, the rancid smell of rotting garbage and human waste in the alleys.

"I think you are in love with Charlie," I blurted out.

"Don't be funny," she retorted, and banged the phone.

I visited her on Christmas day—her mother had called and said I should have lunch with them and she hinted that Malu needed to see me.

It was a memorable day. I brought this engagement ring hoping it would make her happy. It was not much, a simple .32 carat diamond in white gold setting. It was also a bleak day and I did not give her the ring though she gave me a gold-filled ball pen. I couldn't give the ring because for the first time, I saw her cry, the tears just welling in her eyes and down her cheeks.

We were out in the garden by ourselves, under the golden shower pergola. I held her, tried to comfort her. Charlie was dead; they had buried him that morning.

"He had so much promise," she said. He was going back to school so that someday he would be a lawyer and would know how to fight for the "little people" who had no defense; they knew neither the law nor big men.

They were already bulldozing the settlement. The slum dwellers had organized a picket line and Charlie was a leader in the picket. He had left the line to plead with the Metrocom who had now brought the bulldozers. He did not even taunt them. He merely left the line to tell them that all of them, soldiers and squatters alike, were "little people." They shot him instead.

"I ran to him and they would have shot me, too" Malu said, "had the others not rushed with me to the fallen boy."

I was now busy with exams and term papers, but I religiously went to the acacia at noon. Sometimes she joined me, though briefly. At one time, she said she was going to India just to be alone. I remember witnessing a Hindu festival in Singapore: men paraded in the streets, their tongues, their cheeks punctured with long thick needles. A bearded man pulled a cart with ropes fastened to his back muscles by iron hooks. There was no blood and my eyes were not fooling me. It was self-hypnosis again, of this I was sure. Now, serious doubts crowded my mind and I worried about Malu coming back, garbed in saffron and chanting on street corners.

It was during the small graduation dinner Mother gave that I presented the ring to her, told her not to open the package till she got home. That same evening, she called and said she would give it back. I asked why and she said she wanted to be fair with me. She said, "Truly, I love you."

A warm and glorious glow engulfed me. It was the first time she uttered it. Why then give the ring back? I could not understand. How could I compete with something I could not vanquish, least of all touch?

"There is this cause," these were her exact words, "that will take most of my time, my energies, my precious Tengga."

Malu disappeared during the two-month school vacation and frightened her parents and me. Her mother often called to find out if she had gotten in touch. She had gone to the province, she had told her mother, for another of those teach-ins. She would be away for just a couple of weeks, but on the third, when she did not return, we started looking. She had said she would go again to Bicol; I hastily called Uncle Bert, but neither she nor her goup was there. I did not inquire of the army or the constabulary—they were the last people to ask about Malu.

By then, too, I had taken on more responsibilities in our business. I had a desk in Operations and Planning. Mother and my older brothers had thought it best to let me work for a couple of years before going to Wharton for an MBA. It was just as well. I could not concentrate, I brooded over the times Malu and I shared, the conversations and, most of all, that evening in a motel when we held hands and dreamed.

She returned in the first week of June, shortly before classes began. It was her mother who told me she was back. I asked to talk with Malu. Her mother suddenly seemed ill at ease, as if Malu was beside her telling her to say she was not in, for that was what her mother said. I went to her house immediately and was told by the maid who opened the door—she did not let me in—that Malu was still out.

I called again that night and was told she was asleep—although it was only eight. She was avoiding me, she could have easily called. When school opened, I waited for her and this time, there was no escape. She was in the same jeans and formless blouse. She had grown darker and there was a look of unease about her.

"Why don't you want to see me?" I asked bluntly.

She turned around. We were in the vicinity of the registrar's office and students were milling about, looking at bulletin boards, checking their schedules. "I will see you in half an hour at the acacia," she mumbled, her eyes downcast.

"No!" I was angry then. "I will not leave you. I'll follow you till you tell me what is wrong."

She bit her lip. She was in trouble and I wanted to help her, if she would only let me.

We walked out into the street, onward to the library, to our tree. The grass was green now, the dead brown of the dry season banished; the first rains of June had done their job and a freshness perfumed the air. Everything about the world seemed bright, except for this gloom which now encompassed us.

We sat on the old and twisted root. She began slowly. She had no more tears to shed. "They are dead, Teng-ga. All five of them. And I am the only one who got out."

"Who are dead?"

"Bubut, Eddie, Lina, Tom and Alex . . ." She looked at me, beseeched me. I could not quite grasp it at first, but in the back of my mind was a huge, oncoming wave of fear. What had she done? What had she been sucked into?

They had gone to the south, somewhere in the mountains of Quezon, and joined another group for the duration of the school vacation. Familiarization and training, that is what they called it.

On their way back, they had been particularly careful because they were all unarmed. Alex, a medical student, was an old hand and their guide. They bivouacked in an abandoned farmhouse for the night with Alex outside as sentry. That early morning, a shout erupted from the surrounding green ordering them to come out. Even as they filed out of the hut, their hands in the air, they were mowed down.

Malu had dropped quickly to the ground in abject fear and that was how she was spared.

The armed men swarmed around them. A lean man in

jeans, with crew cut, pulled her up from the grass where she was cowering. The men were laughing; they were not in uniform, but they were obviously a commando team. "Leave us alone for a moment," the crew-cut man said, and the men dispersed to the bushes. The man yanked her inside the hut and told her to undress. She begged that she be allowed to look at her friends, they might still be alive, but he just laughed at her. "If they are, we will kill them all before we leave this place. And, of course, we will kill you, too."

She said, "My first thought was one of shame. He started to touch me. I drew away and he barked: 'One more move like that and I will shoot you.' I tried to push him away but he was strong. He was laughing. He held my hands and repeated his threat. I wanted to live. It was painful at first and I thought I would not be able to endure it. But he took his time before he started pushing. I don't know how long it took—I was afraid he would kill me when he got through. I thought I would cooperate so he would let me live. And I started pushing, too. He kissed me and I kissed back. I did! Oh, it was disgusting. He seemed surprised and pleased and he said he would not kill me because I was good, but that if I was not gone in another hour, his men would return and surely use me as he had done, then kill me.

"You just don't know how I hated myself afterwards for doing what I had to do in order to live. Even now, when I remember, I am so ashamed of myself. How can I live with the thought that I am alive, that I was a coward? And after what had happened, I don't want to see you, ever. I have nothing to give you now . . ."

Her hand was cold and trembling. I had listened with anger mingled with sorrow, anger at the men who had killed her friends without reason, at the man who had violated her, and even at Malu herself for having brought this upon herself; sorrow at the wrenching pain that she had to endure and which, I was sure, would scar her always. I wanted to scream at her, but she looked so helpless, like a child who needed sympathy, and I realized it was not just sympathy that I had to give; I loved her truly in a manner I had not realized. I could live with what had happened and help her live, too, if she would let me.

"Plat, the ring which you returned—I would like to give it to you still. I want to marry you. With me, nothing has changed."

THREE

We went to the same motel and decided to get married—"live together" as she put it, with no particular obligations except that we would be faithful to each other. Mother was building a block of duplex apartments in our old compound in Santa Mesa and we could move into the first one finished. She knew of Malu from the beginning and had met her and liked her, but would not approve of the live-in arrangement and neither would her parents. We would lie to them, tell them we had gotten married by a judge in Pasig, that the church wedding would follow after she finished college and we would then leave for the States together.

Because of her trauma, I was prepared to suffer the coldness that she had hinted at. In the apartment, I could sense the tension in her labored breathing, the clamminess in her arms as they encircled me. She tried to be the woman I desired; her kisses, though not passionate, were woman enough, warm enough, and I savored them, gloried in them.

Soon, she began to relax, even to move sensuously. After a time, I throbbed to the strength of her embrace, the quickening thrust of her hips, the contracting and fluttering of her stomach, and the long drawn gasp at the peak—what I was finally giving her, getting from her. When her movements ceased and she came to rest, I drew away to look at her. Her eyes were bright with repressed laughter. I thought I would begin again; I could feel her twitching, pulsing, and roughly, she pushed me away, saying she was so sensitive she could not bear me moving inside her.

She had phoned home and said she'd be away the whole day. We talked far into the night. We had our meals brought in and after brief snatches of sleep, we sought each other again and again. I finally found the completeness that had eluded me all these years.

I promised not to ask what she did during those two months, who her friends were. My ignorance was protection for everyone, she explained. It was she who brought the sad news to the parents of her friends who, like her, lived very comfortably. They never understood why their children gave up their lives so recklessly.

I decided to draw her away from her commitment, to "domesticate" her, make her a mother and tie her to the home or to a normal career, perhaps dreary but safe and never again would she be close to the vortex of death.

I wanted to tell her father about us, but she refused. "I will just move in with you," she said. "But let us draw some rules." She said there would be a time when I would get bored with her. One night a week, I should go out, be on my own, do anything I liked. "Drag to bed any woman—even a whore—and you can tell me if you want to. I will not be angry. I promise. But do not take a mistress, do not get involved with any woman emotionally. And don't bring home any bugs."

I listened to her dumbly.

"Will you permit me to have a night out, too?"

That she asked me at all touched me. I had no choice. "But no affairs," I said.

She nodded. "And someday," she went on, reiterating what she told me earlier, "if we part, it should be as friends."

We moved to Santa Mesa without ceremony. She enjoyed

decorating the two-bedroom apartment. She bought the drapes in Divisoria—light green fabrics that went very well with the furniture. She also bought the appliances and started learning how to "cook Spanish" to please me. I went to her father and we had a long talk. I assured him the church wedding would be very soon. I could tell that he was glad Malu was with me, that I would snatch her away from the crowd that threatened to push her to an anonymous and lonely end. Her mother came and looked at our place. She brought a lot of linens and saw to it that our refrigerator was always stocked. She also sent one of her maids to help, but Malu did not want her to sleep in the apartment; she wanted just the two of us since it was not difficult, she said, to keep house.

My night out was Saturday and hers was Sunday. I felt awkward at first, going out alone, and in time I did see a former girlfriend. I visited my old haunts in Ermita and wandered along the boulevard, but always, a feeling of guilt hounded me as if I was shutting out a part of myself from her, which was not what I wanted for I longed to share everything with her—my time, my possessions. In the end, I gave up going out alone.

She continued, however, to go out every Sunday night. Sometimes, she returned just before daybreak. I would lie awake waiting for the taxi or the car that would bring her home, pretending I was asleep, listening to her undress and finally cuddle close to me, her breath smelling not of wine or of cigarettes but of the same familiar scent. I was curious and jealous every time I heard a man outside saying good night, although sometimes it was a woman, for I always peered out and watched but did not ask.

I went to Cebu every so often to check up on our subsidiary there and called her twice a day, sometimes three, just to hear her voice. If she was not in the apartment, she was in school. Sometimes, we would be unable to connect because she was calling me.

We continued the little debates; I asked her once what her group was doing now and she said, "Don't bother your reactionary head with proletarian politics."

I reminded her again that it was not a crime to be wealthy. I cited how our employees were getting much more than the minimum wage, that they had health and insurance benefits and paid vacations without their asking.

"Paternalism," she said, cutting me short.

No matter, it was a year of blessed happiness which flitted by so quickly that I was hardly aware of the time passing.

I wanted her pregnant so that she would, by force of circumstance, be cut off from all those demonstrations that have now become massive, intermittent, and fraught with danger. All the shops in Ermita were now boarded with plywood and the electric posts and embankments all over downtown Manila screamed with the posters of revolution. Chaos pervaded the universities and classes were haphazard and often suspended.

With my motive urging me on, there was no night that we did not embrace. When a long weekend came, we motored to Baguio. Our house, which we seldom used except during Holy Week or when we had guests, frightened her a bit . . . six rooms upstairs and two downstairs and we were the only occupants because Mang Pedring, the caretaker, and his family had their own quarters above the garage in the rear. We turned on all the lights.

It must have been the Baguio cold, and remembering our first night there afterwards, she said, "*Dios ko,* the whole night. I was never so tired in all my life."

A month after our short vacation, she was pregnant. She could not believe it; she waited for the second month. She consulted three doctors and all the tests were positive. I was ecstatic.

I bought several books on prenatal care and continually asked Mother's advice. Malu's parents were very happy, too, and they often asked when we were finally going to be married in church.

We discussed it once; if we did not get married, her baby would be a bastard. She thought it was very funny, but I did not. "We will have it simultaneously then," she said gaily. "First the wedding, then the baptism."

I looked after her diet carefully and worried that she might start smoking. I told her that whatever she took in, her baby would take it, too. That early, I started buying baby things—diapers, baby powder, safety pins. She said it was all too soon, her stomach did not even show. It was noticeable to me, though, and soon her belt would no longer buckle. She took to wearing larger blouses. She went to school much later and came home earlier. She had cut down some of her activities, even her visits to the *spiritista* chapel in Navotas. But her Sunday evenings were still hers and she kept them all.

One evening, after she had returned from her "free" night out, we talked about the baby's name. I meant it as a joke when I asked, "Are you sure it is mine?"

She glared at me. "Now, what the hell do you mean by that?"

I was still in a joking mood, but I suppose my niggling doubts came through. "Oh, your Sunday nights, you know."

She turned away and in a while, she was shaking violently and when I went to her, sobs were torn out of her in anguish and bitterness. I cradled her in my arms, kissed her hair, assured her that I knew I should not have even hinted that I did not trust her.

I don't really know what happened. She was under expert medical care and I tried my best to make allowances for her moods. Could it be that what I had said bothered her so much? Could it have been caused by the disappearance of many of her friends? At the end of the third month, she started bleeding one afternoon after she got back from school. I rushed her to the hospital where she stayed for a week after she lost her baby, then another two weeks in bed at home to regain her strength before the doctor permitted her to move about.

Now, she was listless and there were times when she was cold to me. I could sense that she was blaming me for the loss. There was milk in her breasts—they were no longer "as small as *kalamansi*." The loss of her baby—it was a boy—was a deep affliction of the soul and I consoled her by saying we could always return to Baguio. We were, as a matter of fact, planning it. I was anxious that she become pregnant again and the doctor said there would be no problem, but that we should be more careful now.

We were to leave that morning. But the papers did not appear and there was no radio either. Something was wrong—so we did not move. When martial law was finally announced on TV, Malu was white-faced. She made some hasty phone calls and talked guardedly. By midday, she said she would go to the university. All she took was her handbag. When she did not return in the afternoon, I called her department. They had not seen her. In the evening, I hurried to Dasmariñas; her parents had not heard from her either. A week later, I received a letter postmarked Manila.

My Precious Teng-ga,

I am very sorry that I had to leave without explanation, without good-bye. Please believe me when I say that I love you and that I will always love you. But duty calls and I have to go. If I don't see you again, just remember that I have always been true. Please forgive me.

Plat

I realized then that she had not abandoned the cause and that it was far more important than I.

Without Malu, I should not have remained in the apartment but I did, hoping she would return. I could not attend fully to our business, but fortunately, we had hired good people. Oh, so many hours alone, going over her books, the papers she wrote, bringing out her clothes, rearranging them in the cabinet—the old and faded jeans, the battered sneakers, and the cotton blouses.

I went to the university. Now, I regretted that I did not know her friends, that I had considered them muddle-headed adolescents unfamiliar with the realities of power—things that an economist or a businessman like myself understood almost as second nature.

Alone, confined to the prison of this skin, this skeletal frame, this net of nerves which relayed nothing but my own despair, I wondered about what I did not know so that I could have restrained her. I was nagged by lassitude, by feelings of worthlessness. Mornings: hard-boiled eggs, sugarless coffee, the prattle of people, the noxious gases of a deadened city, and a vigil in the morgue of evening. I would lie in the dark aching for the phone to ring, a taxi to stop before the house, wondering where she was and the hopes that we had fed on.

Alone, I would wander around Ermita and go to my favorite bar. I never stayed long; the roasted squid and the San Miguel were tasteless, and the jokes I heard were stale. The curfew was an excuse to go home early and though the apartment depressed me, it also sustained me. I developed a tightness in the chest which Dr. Alvarez said was a heart condition that given my youth, I should not have. My legs seemed edemic and my feet were always cold. I was absentminded, I could not function well and I easily forgot names, words, places. I suffered hallucinations and would see things from the corner of my eye which were not really there. Sometimes, I imagined things moving on my desk, the pencil holder, the stapler. Was this what love could do? Its ineffable essence? Malu was right, after all; the mind could afflict the body, too.

Alone, I really had nothing to covet but memories and they came alive at the mere mention of places or names; with them, I was often mesmerized, oblivious to the turmoil around me, the clatter of living. Where could she be now? With whom was she sharing the night? Who was listening to her laughter? Once, driving in Makati, I saw her—or someone like her—hurrying on the sidewalk across the street. I slammed on the brakes, left the car where I had stopped and crossed over, unmindful of the traffic that bore down on me, but when I reached the corner where I thought I saw her, she was gone.

Alone, I sometimes walked the palm-shaded lane by the seawall. The breeze would waft the acrid tang of the sea, now polluted by tidal wash. We had been here several times, usually after visiting Mother in the old Ermita house, and here we watched the sun go down in a splash of reds and golds, waited for the night to take over and the bay and the night above it become one vast blackness sprinkled with stars. All over the world it was dark, so why then could I not live with this gloom? This was the order of things and I should not let it frighten me, intimidate me into thinking that I could not escape it. Her father, after all, had hope and very soon, he would walk in the light again.

I visited the chapel in Navotas. Aling Atang, the priestess, could not tell me where she was other than that she was with friends and that she was always in great danger. But they would try and bring her back. The next time I visited, I could not understand at first when she made-believe and talked to an imaginary Malu with me. She asked how she was, how her father was getting along. She conducted the conversation as if Malu was there answering all her questions.

We went to the prayer meeting and it was the same—all the members acted as if she was with me, as if nothing was wrong. Aling Atang told me afterwards that they had done this every week, prayed as if Malu was in their midst. They would reach out to her and she would then return.

Following their example, I imagined her at the breakfast table, beside me in the car, in bed when I went to sleep. Once the maid who cleaned the apartment and brought the food which Mother always sent, caught me talking alone. She must have thought my mind had snapped for Mother came that evening. She tried to persuade me to return to the house in Ermita.

Like a man with terminal cancer, I was ready to try anything.

Maybe the ritual worked after all. It took an eternity. The fourth year of martial law; one evening in May—I had by then taken to meditation as she had suggested—the phone rang.

"Teng-ga, I am glad I reached you!"

"Plat!" All the nerves in my body sang, my voice a squeak. "Thank God . . ."

"Listen carefully."

"Yes . . . "

"Teng-ga, I owe a friend some money. Can you lend me . . ."

"Of course!"

"Now?"

"Yes!"

"I will be at the acacia in half an hour."

The acacia. I was happy we had a rendezvous about which no one knew. There was no time for me to go to Mother or to her parents. A thousand pesos were in my wallet and about a thousand more were in my drawer. I did not keep money in the apartment and now I wished I did. What else was there of value? The engagement ring which she had left, my watch. I brought them.

I did not even bother putting on shoes. I drove fast, aware that I had little time, filled as I was with joy that I would see her again. See her again! The very thought surged through me, lifted me, I could fly.

The university streets were empty; classes had long ended. I parked, then went down the grassy lawn and on to the tree beyond the library building. When I reached it, there was no one. Had I missed her instructions? Did I hear right? Then in a short while from the shadow of the library, she came. I could not miss her, that height, that build, but she walked slowly as if she was limping.

I rushed to her, kissed her, held her tight and long, smelled the sun on her hair, her face, saw the happiness glistening in her eyes. She was slimmer now and though it was not very bright, I could see she was no longer fair. When I held her hand, I was surprised at how hard and callused it had become.

"Did someone follow you?"

I was in such a hurry that I did not notice, but I was sure no one followed me to the campus.

"Any strangers near the apartment? Any cars you don't recognize parked there?"

I shook my head. "The money," I said, "it may not be enough. I can get more in the morning. But now, I just want to look at you, to hold you. Four years—I have stayed in the apartment alone and waited and waited. Four years . . ." I started to cry.

Her arms tightened around me. "Thank you, my precious Teng-ga." Her voice quavered. "I hope that you have learned to trust me the way I always trusted you. Remember? All those Sunday nights—I was working . . ." She paused and brushed my tears away. "I thought of you, and could not tell you that I was with our group. I know you tried to keep me away from them. I understood."

She did not have to tell me; I had long been convinced of her unblemished constancy. She clasped my hand. "Let us go to the motel again. I need to lie down—even just for a few moments."

"And why not the apartment?"

She did not want to go there; it was dangerous.

I remembered her limp. "Are you hurt?"

"Just a little," she mumbled. "We can talk about other things afterwards."

We walked across the green enveloped by night. A car turned at the far corner and briefly lighted her features. Under the street lamp, she still looked as pretty as ever. I helped her into the car then drove off to Pasay. Once upstairs in the motel, I examined her in the light. She was pale and the brutal life showed in her arms, her face. There was this big blotch on her right thigh. I knew at once what it was.

"You are wounded!"

"It's small," she said, shaking her head.

"Let me see it."

"It will heal when I get back."

"I must find a doctor."

She sat on the bed. "No." she said firmly. "I will be all right."

"You are not all right," I said. "Let me look at it."

She consented after awhile. She lay down with great effort. Around her thigh was a bandage made with her green T-shirt, which she had shredded. She had just a bra beneath her old nylon jacket. The dressing—poorly done and locked with a safety pin—was drenched with dried blood. Beneath was a deep wound which cut across her thigh, the beautiful thigh that I had often caressed, still fair, unlike her lower limbs which were dark with sun and specked with insect bites.

"I was able to run," she said, breathing deeply. "So I was able to call you. I just had a few coins for the phone and the bus."

I carefully put the bandage back. "It must hurt a lot," I said hoarsely, my throat gone dry. She did not reply. Physical pain was not her worry now.

She had to be in the hospital immediately. There was the possibility of infection and the wound had to be closed. She had to have a transfusion, too. But I could not take her to a hospital and to call a doctor to the motel was out of the question. The apartment—that was the best place. In the years that I was alone, I had noticed nothing unusual. I was now keen to the possibility that the house would be watched, but I was positive this was not done. No one knew of the acacia, and I doubted if any of her friends or mine knew our private nicknames.

"I will bring you to the apartment where you will stay until you are strong again. " Then, I said it and was surprised how easily the words came. "I will go with you now, wherever you will go."

Her eyes misted. She was tired and in pain and did not argue anymore. God, I don't know how long she had endured it.

"You know best," she said weakly, then passed out.

I was amazed at my self-control. After I had calmly phoned

the desk that we were leaving, I carried her down to the car, wondering if Dr. Alvarez, who was a family friend, would be at home, and who would be a good alternative if he was not available.

She revived when we reached the highway and she snuggled close, whimpering like a child.

Who was it who said that we all hurt the ones we love? With Malu, I did not hurt her; I killed her. Why did I have to bring her home?

We were going up the incline toward the compound when a car blocked our way. It must have been with her last reserve of strength that she swung the door open and sprinted out, limping, and to the men who had rushed out of their cars, guns drawn, I shouted "Don't shoot! She is wounded! She cannot run!"

Flashes of fire spurted from the snouts of their guns and the bullets winked like fireflies as they hit the asphalt. Malu, my dear wife, crumpled and even when she was already dead, they still fired at her.